Aunt Jane-Ann
Takes a Holiday

By

Jennifer Cadgwith

Copyright

Acknowledgments

Thank you to those of you who have offered encouragement, support, and suggestions for this novel. You know who you are.

A special thank you to Jeff Totaro, Mary Totaro, and Catherine Buzbee.

I have found out that there ain't no surer way to find out whether you like people or hate them than to travel with them.

— Mark Twain
Tom Sawyer Abroad

Chapter One

May 2019

"Put your phone down, Jessie. The teapot's empty, and the bacon's going to burn if you don't pay attention. We'll hear something soon enough, but I hope Jackson gets Jane-Ann through Customs all right," my boyfriend Beckham Hailey said to me over breakfast at Lilac House, my beloved seventeenth-century Cotswolds residence near Broadway, Worcestershire.

Boyfriend. Beck was my boyfriend, I thought as I got up to check the bacon and grab the kettle that was boiling on the black Aga cooker. I dropped a couple of Irish Breakfast teabags into my great-grandmother Jenson's floral-patterned, porcelain teapot on the table before pouring in the water.

The term 'boyfriend' was such an odd way for a forty-nine-year-old woman to think of the man who sat at the kitchen table, but we weren't really partners. He didn't live with me; he couldn't. He had a job in London. While I could write my novels anywhere, I didn't want to permanently reside in the Belgravia townhouse that belonged to my late husband's family, and especially not with my boyfriend, partner, or whatever anyone wanted to call him. As far as living in his flat, it wasn't ideal. Besides the place being a bit small for two, I didn't want the inevitable gossip upsetting my mother-in-law.

Letting the tea steep, I drained the streaky bacon, piled it on a white plate, and set it on the old, round, oak kitchen table. After I was once again seated, I poured myself a fresh cup of tea and thought about Beck's comment before answering. Would there be trouble with my aunt entering the country? It wouldn't surprise me.

My aunt, Jane-Ann Simmons, was not the easiest person with whom to deal, and she was arriving in London early this afternoon. I'd surprised her with a trip for her birthday. To be honest, part of the reason was that I felt guilty that she had no family left in Hilly Dale since my mother died and I'd returned to England.

"Are you listening to me, Jessie?" Beck asked.

"Jackson's with her, and he knows the drill well enough. Besides, we flew them here on a private jet to make her more comfortable. It's her first flight anywhere," I replied, watching Beck as he took several pieces of bacon and placed them on his plate "And they're being driven to the townhouse."

"Yeah, that was probably a wise move. She'll be the toast of the town after she returns home to Hilly Dale, Arkansas," he said, his dark-blue eyes twinkling. "Her stories about visiting you should get her more invitations than she dreamed possible."

"It's not like my life is a secret anymore." I eschewed the milk and took a sip of tea. After all my years in England, I had never been able to tolerate milk in my tea. I took it straight and strong, and sometimes that garnered me questioning looks, and the occasional whisper of *American* by some of my set – my set being the nobility. My late husband was William Fielding-Smythe, Duke of Hearthe, and that made me a duchess. I might not be *the* duchess now that my stepson Alistair was married, but since I had not remarried, I still held my rank.

"I think she'll be in for a shock." Beck finished his scrambled eggs before continuing, "I mean, someone can hear your accent and look at the pictures, but until one is actually with you in your element, one doesn't have a clue to what your life is like here. I was in awe when I saw how you lived. I'm getting used to it, but it's still amazing to me how you ended up a duchess."

"I like how you've taken to using the pronoun 'one,'" I said. "As to *what* you said, a duchess is who and what I am. Well, that and being an author. I realized that during my time in Hilly Dale."

"You'll have to remind Jane-Ann to call you 'Carola,' in certain circumstances, and she's going to make a fuss about that." Beck bit into the bacon and washed it down with a sip of coffee. Despite having re-located indefinitely to England with his job six months ago, he was not tea-crazy at all. When he visited my family at Fielding House, the butler Mr. Bailing – I refused to address him by just his last name – tried not to roll his eyes. Mr. Bailing was anti-coffee.

"Good thing you'll be there to remind her when she arrives," I replied, adding, "You can help her remember my name by remembering to use it yourself, when appropriate. Be glad that Alistair doesn't stand on a great deal of formality, like my late father-in-law."

"You'll always be Jessie to me. I'm not going to be around Jane-Ann much. Some of us have to work. By that, I mean work at a real office." Beck worked for Courtney Hazelforth, an investment firm that had offices in New York City and London. He'd been going back and forth but finally applied for a transfer and had gotten it.

"I work. I write novels. *Stars and Spikes Forever* in *The Celestial Cat* cozy mystery series ranked high on all the lists, and all the *Harriet Donovan* novels are doing extremely well," I replied, unable to resist responding to his taunt.

"Since the world found out that well-known author Jessica Keasden was really Carola, Duchess of Hearthe, which your publisher pushed the hell out of, you *should* be doing well," he teased. "You need to catch up on that new series, though. You're dropping the ball there."

"Very funny. I cranked out three of the *Secrets of Snowdonia* series in the past year-and-a-half. I don't like to write that fast, and I still owe another *Harriet*. I simply don't have an idea for it, yet."

"Whatever you say, Duchess." Beck pushed back his chair, stood up, walked over to me, and kissed the top of my head. "Going for a walk while you finish getting ready. I need to prepare myself for your aunt. She's going to hammer away at me for not marrying you. Maybe I'll just tell her why that is."

Beck enjoyed badgering me, just like he did when we met in seventh-grade. We'd parted company at the beginning of tenth, due to the manipulation of the woman who later in life tracked him down and married him. Other than their lovely daughter Jordan who was now dating my son Liam, their marriage had been a mistake. The fact that our children were involved was part and parcel of my complicated life with Beck. It was one of the reasons we were not contemplating marriage. And I most certainly could not have continued 'dating' Beck in Hilly Dale had I chosen to remain there, especially after news of my title was discovered. There would have been no privacy. There would also have been too much speculation and, of course, 'encouragement' from my aunt.

Hilly Dale was not a bad place. It was just not a fit for me. In all fairness, when I moved to the small town, I was not in a particularly good frame of mind. I was looking to escape the life I'd been leading in Hearthestone Vale after my husband died. There were too many memories everywhere I looked, and nothing in the family residences was mine, so I suppose I was open to adventure and a new life in my hometown where I'd inherited my childhood home. Instead of the life I envisioned, I went from the frying pan into the fire, memories-wise, and that included the moment I bumped into Beckham Hailey at the local Walmart.

As time passed, Beck and I connected, but I found myself becoming increasingly distressed to learn that Hilly Dale wasn't what I thought it was, but perhaps as an adult who had lived elsewhere and traveled extensively I was seeing the town through different eyes. It took a dramatic situation involving a former friend and classmate to help me realize where I belonged, where I was truly happy, and who I was, and it was not in America.

For Beck, though, it had taken a great deal more to realize what he wanted, make the sacrifices, and to come after it. I often wondered if he'd made the right choice moving to London. If his daughter hadn't been in university in England, I doubted he would have moved. I didn't know what would happen once she finished school next term.

I heard the front door close with a thud. A ramble down the lane and into the village of Broadway, even if we didn't need anything, was something he both enjoyed while he was visiting me, and we often strolled into the village on a Saturday morning to do marketing or stop for tea and coffee. It was often easier and faster to walk than to take the car and find a parking spot what with the tourists about. I put the dishes in the dishwasher and set the timer before glancing at the clock on the wall. *Oh my God!*

Staring down at my plush black bathrobe and bare feet, I realized I was going to have to hurry to be ready by the time he returned. I needed to shower, dress, and finish packing. It wasn't terribly far, but from experience, I knew to allow two-and-a-half hours to reach Belgravia by car. You just never knew about the traffic, and I did *not* want my aunt and Jackson to arrive at the townhouse first! My aunt would be appalled if I wasn't there to greet them.

As I climbed the worn stairs, I heard Violet, my black Persian cat, howling from an upstairs bathroom where she'd been confined. Violet, like most pets, instinctively picked up on the fact that she was headed to the veterinarian. Dr. Collie – yes, that was his name - was boarding her at the clinic for the nearly three weeks I'd be gone. While Violet was welcome at the townhouse, she was less so at Fielding House. It was her old home, but now that there was a new duchess living there, animals in the house were not appreciated. In fact, they weren't appreciated at all. I hated to leave my sweet cat behind, but I had faith in Dr. Collie. He and his staff provided excellent care, and fussy Violet seemed to like them well enough, after her usual upon-arrival hissy-fit.

***

"About ready to go?" Beck asked, walking into the bedroom an hour later and flopping on the seventeenth-century bed's rose-brocade duvet.

"*About* being the operative word," I replied, closing my navy-blue, leather tote bag.

"You're dressed, and that's a good start." He took in my cream-colored trousers and indigo silk blouse with the bell sleeves. "You're pretty dressed-up for a ride into London."

"My aunt wouldn't expect me to be there in a pair of jeans, plaid shirt and a baseball cap," I retorted, looking at his attire. "She'd think that was too casual for a duchess. Toss me my jacket, please."

"Hey, I'm not staying. I'll greet her and go on to my flat," Beck threw the dark-blue and white striped jacket at me, which, thankfully I caught. "You'll have Jackson to run interference while she's here," he said, getting off the bed, walking over to me, and ruffling my hair.

"I just brushed it. That's going to take more time to re-do," I complained, looking in the mirror over the chest-of-drawers.

Beck just laughed and ruffled it again. "Need anything else before I take stuff to the car?"

"I still need to get the things for William Charles for when we go to Fielding House. The presents are in the guest room. Would you please take them downstairs for me? I'll be there in a few minutes."

"You're taking *this* much stuff! You planning to spend a couple of months?"

"Well, Jackson and my aunt will be here longer than most visitors, so while he's off exploring on his own, I'll be taking my aunt to whatever she wants to see, and there *is* the party, so I'll need formal wear. Aunt Jane-Ann may be going on eighty-two, but she's in good health, and you know how active she is. She tries to walk each day in her neighborhood, and she balked at my suggestion that she take the downstairs bedroom my parents used at their house when they got older."

Aunt Jane-Ann lived in my childhood home. She'd always coveted the Jenson family's large, white Victorian house which overlooked part of Hilly Dale's downtown, and since I was returning to England permanently, I didn't need it, so it made perfect sense to deed it to her. She wasn't a Jenson, but her sister – my mother - married one, so it was still sort of in the family.

I looked in the mirror again. Crap! Beck had really mussed me up. My aunt would point out that my hair looked like a rat's nest. She was pickier than my mother-in-law Josephine – the oldest Duchess of Hearthe. I took a moment to run a brush through my shoulder-length, light brown hair that had been freshly highlighted with blonde last week in London. Grabbing a lipstick, I touched up the rose color I was wearing. Just as I was about to visit the lavatory one last time, I heard Beck call from the bottom of the stairs, "Let's go!"

"Violet?"

"I've got her."

"The presents?"

"Got 'em. Let's go!"

"You have all my bags?"

"YES! Do you see them up there?"

"No."

"I repeat, LET'S GO!"

"My," I said, while locking up the house, "you're in a hurry to see my aunt."

"No, I just don't want to face her wrath if you aren't there to greet her," he replied voicing my earlier thought.

"You're just cranky because you decided to come see me after work yesterday and now we're going back to London today. You didn't get much rest."

"Yeah, I should have thought that through, but we won't have much time together while Jane-Ann and Jackson are here."

"At least I've got a driver today."

Beck was driving but we were taking my new car, a 2019 black BMW 750. It was roomy enough for everyone and could hold all the luggage, and it was an automatic shift, which I loved. I'd purchased it myself – another reason I loved it. My 1960 XK150 special-order silvery-gray Jaguar convertible, part of the Fielding-Smythe collection, was parked in the converted stable at the back of the house. It was my running-around car, or maybe my show-off car. It had been mine to use for many years.

"Don't forget to lock the gate," I cried as we exited Lilac House's private drive."

"You say that every time we leave. Look, I'm clicking the button now. You have a real thing for fences and gates, Jessie. Before I moved to New York City, people in Hilly Dale were still talking about the black iron fence around your house. I wonder if your aunt still has it up."

"Something for you to ask her then," I replied, smiling.

Chapter Two

"Well, I never," Aunt Jane-Ann declared before she even said 'Hello' or I had a chance to welcome her. Marching past me into the London townhouse's foyer, she cast her eyes around the room, taking in the polished marble floor, the crystal chandelier, and the mahogany staircase, finally settling her gaze not on me but on Mrs. Herren the housekeeper and general caretaker of the Belgravia residence. Mr. Herren who acted as butler and chauffeur was bringing in the luggage. ""My this *is* grand," my aunt said.

"I told you so," Jackson Barker, my dearest friend from Hilly Dale stated, rolling his eyes at me. "But you didn't believe me, Jane-Ann."

"Who would? A private jet, a Rolls Royce to bring us to this house..."

"In an exclusive area of London, too," Jackson enthusiastically interrupted. "And it was a Bentley, not a Rolls."

My aunt looked over her silver-rimmed glasses and wrinkled her nose at the history professor with whom she'd just crossed the Atlantic Ocean."

"If you say so, Jackson," she snipped. "You were extremely *informative* on our drive here."

"I do, and I was."

"Welcome to London, Aunt." I gave her a hug, followed by a kiss on the cheek. "And Jackson." I embraced him tightly while whispering in his ear, "Did everything go all right?"

"Lots to tell," he murmured just before we separated. "Beckham, wonderful to see you. How do you like living in London?"

Beck, who had been leaning awkwardly against a polished marquetry hall table came forward and shook hands with the retired history professor. "It's different, but there are perks residing here." He glanced at me and smiled.

"I'm sure you would both like to rest a bit," I said quickly to cover my embarrassment. "Mrs. Herren, would you please show Mrs. Simmons to her room. I'm sure you would both prefer to use the lift."

The townhouse had a brass cage-style lift that had been installed decades ago. After having been stuck in it once, I refused to use it.

"Certainly, Your Grace," Mrs. Herren replied. From the corner of my eye, I caught my aunt's stunned expression.

"Thank you. That would be most agreeable," my aunt replied, sounding like she'd stepped out of a Merchant-Ivory film...until she spotted Beck with Jackson, and reverted to her old self, blurting, "Beckham, where do you stay here?"

"Uh...ummm...uh," Beck stammered and ran his fingers through his silver-tinged dark hair. "I, uh..."

"Beckham has a flat in Chelsea, but if he didn't, he would have his own room as do all guests at Fielding-Smythe properties," I stated, stopping the direction my aunt was headed with her question, and in front of the Herrens too! "You and Jackson, Aunt, will be staying on the same floor as I. This answers the question about room assignments, I trust." I gave her a very sweet smile, hoping it reached my eyes.

Beck never shared a room with me at any of the Fielding-Smythe properties, with the exception of Lilac House, but that was, essentially, *my* residence and we were alone there. I would never embarrass my family by bringing my boyfriend to visit and expect them to accept our sleeping arrangements.

"I've got to go," Beck said, edging toward the front door. Mr. Herren beat him to it and stood holding the door open. "I'll see you at Fielding House. If you talk to Liam, tell him I said to not get involved with any Scottish lasses. I don't want him breaking my daughter's heart."

Knowing Beck was teasing, I smiled, but Alistair *had* sent Liam to the Highlands a couple of days ago to look at cattle he was interested in purchasing. After that, Liam was going to check out several possible investment properties. Catching up with Beck, just outside the door, we said our goodbyes. We never kissed in public, and I certainly didn't want to start now with my aunt possibly peering around the door frame.

"Well, let's get you to your room, Jackson. It's the one you had last time. Mr. Herren will take you," I said when I returned.

A few minutes later I met Mrs. Herren outside the door to my aunt's room. "I apologize for my aunt's comment about sleeping arrangements a few moments ago. She's a tad blunt."

"I understand, Your Grace. There will be a light lunch in half-an-hour. Mrs. Helms is here today."

Mrs. Helms was a woman from a catering service Alistair had recently hired to prepare meals when someone was in residence and brought guests. There was no need otherwise. Mrs. Herren would cook or we went out for meals, other than breakfast.

"Thank you," I replied, smiling at the dark-haired woman who was only slightly older than I. Mrs. Herren and her husband had been with the family for ten years. After she disappeared down the stairs, I bravely knocked on my aunt's door before entering.

"Don't you wait for a 'come in' or 'enter,' Jessica? It's rude to barge in someone's room. What if I'd been in a state of undress?"

God forbid, I'd have hated to see that!

"I apologize. I assumed since Mrs. Herren just left you were still dressed. Members of our staff tend to knock and then enter, except for the bedrooms and lavatories. Are you pleased, Aunt?" I asked, watching her run a finger over the top of the early nineteenth-century dresser.

"Excellent housekeeping, Jessica. Not a speck of dust. I even checked under the bed with my cane and there are no dust bunnies, but I've yet to check the bathroom. Dirt and dust around the toilet are indicators of poor housekeeping."

Trust my aunt to notice those details the minute she arrived in her bedroom at an elegant London townhouse. I doubted she'd find dirt or dust around the toilet. Mrs. Herren hired cleaners from a very reputable agency.

"I'm happy it meets your specifications. I certainly hope you will be comfortable."

"I think I might be. I must say I was stunned when you invited me here, especially since I didn't have an invitation to your wedding or to my nephew's."

Not this again. She knew very well why no one from the States but my parents attended my wedding. It was decided that it was in my parents' best interests that who I married be kept secret from those in my hometown, and Aunt Jane-Ann, who was not known for being silent, would have told 'just one person' and it would have gone from there. As for Alistair's wedding, it was never even considered.

"You're here now," I replied, already wondering if this had been a mistake after all.

"I don't know what to say except thank you for this lovely trip. I can't get over it. A private jet! A Rolls? Or was it a Bentley like Jackson said?"

"Bentley," I confirmed. "And, you're welcome. I hope you have a nice time."

"Such luxury! I see why those like you travel this way."

Contrary to what she imagined we did not travel by private jet often. When I lived in Hilly Dale, my aunt developed some sort of fixation with private jets after she learned I'd traveled on them. She'd often referred to them, as well as my 'hobnobbing' with royalty. While I doubted there would be any real hobnobbing going on, there *were* other things I had planned I knew she would enjoy. I made a quick decision to tell her.

"I was going to surprise you, but perhaps it's best you know now."

"You're pregnant!" she screeched. "A woman of *your* age! You're a *grandmother* now! Grandmother's don't get pregnant, Jessica. Oh I know these change-of-life babies happen, but you're not *married* to Beckham. It *is* his, correct? Or is there some earl or another duke you're seeing as well?"

I'd say I was shocked and couldn't believe I was hearing this, but I could. Beck's marital status had been of the utmost concern to my aunt when I was in Arkansas. There, it had been that I was seeing a married man – never mind he was getting a divorce and hadn't lived with his soon-to-be ex for two years, and during that time she had been flaunting an affair with a man named John Knoss. Now that Beck had moved across the Atlantic to be with me, she was upset we hadn't married. Worse, she now assumed that I was pregnant and that there might be another contender for the father!

With indignation, I raised my voice, "NO. I'm not pregnant. Be serious."

"Well, it happens…my friend's *aging* daughter just had a baby and the father is unknown. He's some sperm donor. Part of that baby came from a cup in a clinic where the donor…"

"Monday, you, my friend Elsie, and I are going to The Chelsea Flower Show," I said quickly to stop the discussion of sperm banks and cups.

Aunt Jane-Ann began to sway, nearly toppling over. "The Chelsea Flower Show? *I'm* going *there*? Oh my goodness. I need to sit down. That's a dream come true. Not one of my garden club friends has been to *that*. Oh, Margaret has been to Sissinghurst, but she hasn't been to the Chelsea."

"Margaret?"

"You met her, Jessica. Really, you paid no attention to people in Hilly Dale. We had lunch with her at The Old House Restaurant. You should know *that* place well, or maybe it was just Beck's apartment upstairs. I remember Margaret was wearing a blue cardigan that day. It's her favorite."

Ah, Lady Cornflower. "I believe I do remember her. I met her another time at Cobble's market. She seemed very intent upon telling me about her visit to Sissinghurst and about the Sackville-Wests. Oh, and you really must remember to call me 'Carola' here, at least in certain situations. Not when we're alone or with family, of course."

"Well, your name to me is Jessica, but you *certainly* are not Jessie Jenson any longer, so I'll try to…Carola. I thought I'd collapse when I heard that woman refer to you as 'Your Grace.' Just like on those PBS shows. And Jackson told me this house is in the neighborhood from *Upstairs, Downstairs.* I bought the DVDs some time ago. Do you think we could go to Eaton Place?"

"This townhouse is in Eaton Square, but it's not Eaton Place."

"My word! I'm in Eaton Square. I have to see where the series was filmed."

"It's not really 165 Eaton Place, Aunt. It's 65 Eaton Place that was used for the exterior shots, but I'll take you there if you like. You can't go inside. It's been turned into flats, I believe."

"I want a photo of me standing in front."

"I'm not sure that's a good idea, but I'll hire a driver to take us about London tomorrow so you can sightsee, and you can take photos from the open car window if there isn't a parking spot near what you wish to visit. How's that?"

"Car?"

"Yes, there's a lot of walking in London, and speaking of that, it will be the same at the flower show," I warned. "Are you up to that?"

"Of course I'm up to it. I'd crawl buck-naked over the rocks near Dagnabbit Creek in Hilly Dale – and you know some of those rocks are sharp - if only to get one over on Margaret. Margaret's daughter is the one who got her baby's father from the sperm bank," she repeated herself, but added, "I just hope he's smart because Margaret's daughter is dumber than a box of…"

"The plan is to spend a couple of days here, go to Cornwall, on to Hearthestone Vale and Fielding House, then back to London for a couple of days," I interrupted.

"Cornwall? Oh, I know that from *Poldark* and *Doc Martin.*"

"There's that, of course," I said, wondering when she had become so interested in PBS programs, "but there is also The Eden Project which I thought you would enjoy, and I'm *certain* not one of your garden club members has been *there*! Think of the programs you could present at meetings, Aunt Jane-Ann."

"You don't have to sell me on Cornwall, Jessica, but what is this Eden Project?"

"Biomes – domed spaces containing thousands of plants. There's a rainforest that's supposed to be spectacular, and in it there is a waterfall. Since it will have a tropical climate inside, we'll want to dress in layers. Cornwall itself can be unpredictable, by the way. I was there once in August and there was nothing but cold rain for several days. It's the third week in May and the Hearthestone Vale area may be chilly to you, too. It's not like May in Arkansas."

"I brought my cardigans, my rain hat, umbrella, and shoe covers. The Eden Project will do," she proclaimed. "Are there flowering plants? Beautiful flowers?"

"I've never been, but yes, there will be flowers."

"While we're in Cornwall, could we *visit* the locations where *Doc Martin* is filmed? It's so pretty there."

"Port Isaac? Our Cornish house, Trevenston Manor, is not far from there." I stopped, stunned by my ease of talking about Cornwall. While Cornwall was renowned for its beautiful scenery and history, and the area where the manor was located was steeped in both, it was a place I'd *never* wanted to visit again after my husband died at sea during a sailing event off the coast. Beck had once told me I needed to face the place again, so I suppose it was best to do so when I'd be occupied with a friend and family member. *Doc Martin* country, Boscastle, and the Tintagel Castle ruins were in the area, so that might be a good way to keep busy.

"And can we see where *Poldark* is filmed?"

"I suppose so, if we have time. Some of the locations are not too far a drive, but please, Aunt Jane-Ann, keep in mind that we aren't traveling on American interstate highways to most of these places so it will take longer, and Cornwall is a popular holiday destination, even now, which means the traffic can be heavy at times."

"And what about some of the places used in *Victoria?*" she asked, not listening to a word I said.

I tried not to sigh, but a small one escaped. "Weren't we talking about Cornwall and where you would like to go?"

"We were, but now that I think about it, I'd like to see some of the other locations from programs I enjoy."

"We're not going to be in the area where some of the exteriors for *Victoria* are filmed." All that was missing was for her to ask to go to Highclere Castle and take a tour of all the other locations used in *Downton Abbey*, but we weren't going to be in that area either. At least she hadn't asked to tour Buckingham Palace. That I could not do for her; the Queen was in residence at this time.

"If you like, we might visit Westminster Abbey before you return to Arkansas. It's quite something to see, and, of course there are many other..." I let the sentence trail.

"You're in charge."

THAT was a first!

"Mrs. Herren said lunch would be ready in," I looked at my watch, "about fifteen minutes, unless you would prefer to rest."

"No, I can rest at home. I'm here to see things…and to visit with you." Aunt Jane-Ann stood up, straightened her hair, and said, "Lead on."

Lunch was served in the small dining room – the larger, formal one was reserved for dinner parties. Jackson, already seated, stood as we entered. "Ladies," he said, "join me for this delightful meal."

Mrs. Helms had prepared consommé, sandwiches, salad, and small cakes.

"This is more like an afternoon tea. It's not time for that," Aunt Jane-Ann stated firmly and looked at her watch. "Don't you follow the custom?"

"Yes, you are correct, but with your long trip, I thought you might prefer to have a light lunch instead, and then if you are hungry later we will have dinner. Jackson, if you prefer to dine out tonight, you certainly may. Mr. Herren will make reservations for you."

"No, unlike Jane-Ann, I didn't get much sleep on the way over, so I'll have an early night. Tomorrow, I plan to take in the museums. I haven't been in a while. "

"Was the plane not comfortable?"

"Oh, it was wonderful. It was just a bit noisy." Glancing at Aunt Jane-Ann who was selecting a sandwich from the tray, he mouthed, "She snored."

"Well, I found the flight delightful. I must have slept like a baby because the next thing I knew, we were arriving in London."

Jackson gave her a sardonic look and dipped a spoon into the chicken consommé.

Chapter Three

The moment I was heading for the lavatory to indulge in a long, hot, relaxing shower, someone knocked on my bedroom door. Looking at the bedside clock, I groaned. 8:30 p.m. Expecting to find my aunt in a cardigan and nightgown, I was more than surprised to find Jackson standing there in his tartan pajamas, navy bathrobe, and slippers.

"What's the matter?" I asked.

"This was the first opportunity I had to speak with you privately."

"Come in. Have a seat," I said indicating a taupe brocade chair under a window. Pulling my robe tightly around me, I curled up in the matching one just across from him. "Shoot."

"You don't know how good that word sounds to me, at the moment. Jane-Ann was beside herself before we left. She told the *Hilly Dale Gazette* she would have photos and information for Gatsby Gregson about the trip. The paper's owner, well, you know him, Peter Franklin, has offered to *pay* for them. You had better be careful what she hears, what she sees, where you take her, and what you do."

Oh, dear. I knew Gatsby Gregson somewhat, but I knew Peter Franklin's wife well. Betsy Potter Franklin had been the bane of my existence in high school, and all because her friend Bianca had lied and manipulated Beck into breaking up with me in tenth-grade so she could date him. Betsy, unlike Bianca, had matured into a decent person and now helped Jackson oversee the renovations being made to the downtown, which were due to the ten-million dollars I'd set aside for that purpose when I left.

"Do you mean Peter's having her spy on my family and me?" I was stunned.

"No, nothing that nefarious. He wants something more like a travelogue, but Jane-Ann now considers herself a reporter, and you need to be careful what she reports. She has a tendency to…uh…embellish certain things."

How well, I knew *that*. While I lived in Hilly Dale, she'd told the paper I wore gorgeous jewels while wandering around an ancient

English manor. After letting out a long sigh, which was something I did frequently when it came to my aunt, I finally said, "I suppose it doesn't matter now that I don't live there, but I'd rather false information not be spread again."

"Jane-Ann's enjoying the house, Jessica. I think living there has turned her head even more. She's made it to the pinnacle of Hilly Dale society, and after this vacation she'll have the big-head."

"Beck said something similar this morning, but I'm glad it's made her happy. Something else I've discovered about her. She's been in the closet."

Jackson cleared his throat. "Uh…in the closet? What do you mean?"

"She's hooked on PBS. Public Broadcasting. Channel 13 in Hilly Dale. So far, she wants to see where the *Upstairs, Downstairs* exterior is and mentioned that in Cornwall, she wanted to see where *Doc Martin* was filmed, and have we the time, she wants to go to *Poldark* country, and she's asked about visiting *Victoria* locations!"

"I know. She babbled a lot about *Downton Abbey* to me. I suppose she chose two of the places because they were in Cornwall. She asked if we would be near Highclere Castle. I said, that we would not. Thank you. I wouldn't mind if we had more time, but one has to pick and choose."

"Since you left, she's been on an 'English kick' in Hilly Dale. She's hosted several high teas. Had them catered by the bakery. The women come dressed in hats and gloves. *Gloves!* I was only invited to one so that I could speak on Alistair and Cecilia's wedding. I didn't give out a great deal of information, much to the attendees' disappointment, but I did talk about the clothes and the tiaras. That was a hit, and, of course meeting Prince Harry. Some of the women swooned. *Swooned*, Jessica!"

Changing the subject, I asked, "How are the downtown renovations going?"

"Very well. There were plenty of people begging for the funds, and, of course, the mayor let it slip you were the benefactress, but I assumed they would figure it out."

"It's important to preserve downtown history, and I felt it was being neglected in favor of more modern buildings away from the center of town."

"Timothy Hayes didn't agree at all. His nose is completely out-of-joint." Timothy Hayes was the president of Hilly Dale College.

"Oh?"

"My, yes. He was expecting you to leave a large endowment to the college since your daughter Aisling attended for one semester. *One semester* and he expected millions!"

"He didn't want to help or even entertain the thought of revitalizing the downtown by utilizing the buildings there. He told me so. He was looking for outside property on which to build. Now he is complaining because I thought the old buildings had merit and deserved to be renovated and thus chose to spend *my* money as *I* saw fit? That sounds about right."

"How are your children?" Jackson saved me from a rant.

"Liam graduated from Cambridge with a first and has been working for Alistair. He's in Scotland on business. You probably heard Beck allude to that before he left. Aisling is still at St. Andrews. The term isn't over, but she will join us at Fielding House for the party. Keep the party a secret, please."

Jackson made a zipping motion across his lips.

"Alistair and Cecilia are adjusting to being parents, and William Charles is adorable. His nanny is a jewel. About the party, though, I'm going all out with formal attire. Don't worry if you haven't a tux with you. We'll find one. It is Aunt Jane-Ann's eighty-second and she has made such a to-do about not being invited to my wedding, I thought something formal would be nice for her. And since you mentioned she's been having teas, this should be a highlight. She may want to host black-tie events after this, though."

"Oh, Lord! She will be over the moon. Think how she can brag to her friends! And you and Beckham? Any news on that front?"

"You sound like my aunt." I told him what she'd said and then about Lady Cornflower's daughter.

Jackson guffawed. "*Aging* women and talk about using a cup for a sperm donation? And it's the prim, proper Jane-Ann in her cardigan calmly discussing this intimate subject? I can't believe it!"

"Believe it. It's one of those things you never expect someone to say right after they arrive as a houseguest, and you certainly don't want to know this information about someone they know either. Worse, she thought I was pregnant and it might not be Beck's."

"On that fascinating note, I'm off to bed. Looking forward to a full day immersed in the museums."

***

The Chelsea Flower Show, arguably the *premier* flower show in the world, was held on the south grounds of the Royal Hospital. After Sunday's private tour of London and my aunt wanting to hop in and out of the hired car for pictures, I was glad that my best friend Elsie was joining us today. Something I did not share with my aunt was that this was the flower show's "Press Day" – a VIP day during which royalty and celebrities attended. Because I was Duchess of Hearthe and my friend Elsie was the Vicountess Toddle, we had been invited and had managed to get my aunt included.

I dressed carefully in a floaty brown and white patterned, calf-length dress with a thin brown leather belt, stepped into fashionable, but comfortable, nude, low-heeled pumps, grabbed a small, emerald green Mulberry handbag by its handle, and went to check on my aunt.

"Aunt Jane-Ann?" I called through her bedroom door. "Breakfast will be ready. Are you dressed?" No answer. I knocked and turned the knob. The room was empty; the bed was carefully made. "Aunt Jane-Ann?" I called and tapped on the bathroom door. I was met with silence.

When I entered the dining room, I found her staring blankly at Jackson from across the table. "Aunt, are you all right?"

She said nothing.

"Aunt Jane-Ann," I cried, walking over to her and touching her shoulder. "Are you all right?"

"Oh, yes. Jackson just told me about today. Will Queen Elizabeth really be there? Will I get to see Her Majesty? Meet her?"

I gave Jackson a look that screamed, 'Why?' While I knew it would come out eventually today, I didn't expect it to be at breakfast.

"Well, Jane-Ann was going to find out soon enough. I remember how I didn't know Prince Harry was going to be at Alistair's wedding. And then at the reception, I worried I'd make a fool of myself if I had a chance to meet him. I wanted Jane-Ann to be prepared."

Taking a seat next to him, I heard him mutter "and not make a scene at the show."

"Thanks," I said. "Her Majesty tends to arrive later in the day, but you might see her from a distance at some point. It's highly doubtful we will speak to her, or anyone else in the family. You *will* see celebrities there, and my friend Elsie who is picking us up is a viscountess."

"That's a much lower rank. *You* are a duchess. I would think you would be on good terms with the Royal Family. The Prince of Wales was at your wedding and your husband's service, after all. Prince Harry was at Alistair's wedding..."

"Oh, we are on good terms in a way. I am just personally not well-acquainted with Her Majesty, or most of the members of the family. I have met them through social engagements over the years, of course, and the younger royals through my sons, but I certainly do not know them well-enough to run up and say, 'How dee do?' That is not done."

"Well, that certainly is disappointing, but understandable. I shall stay on the fringes and I most certainly will enjoy the gardens."

"Oh, you will. I've been several times. I'm a member of the Royal Horticultural Society, and so is..."

Oh. My. God. What had I just said? The RHS was a tradition in the Fielding-Smythe family and since my mother-in-law could no longer go, and Cecilia had no interest in performing 'boring duchess duties,' as she called them, I still represented the family at certain things. The Chelsea Flower Show was one of them, and now I'd outed myself.

"*You're* a member of that prestigious organization and you have been several times to The Chelsea Flower Show, yet you wouldn't join

Hilly Dale Garden Club? Jessica, that is snobbish and it's very insulting. You said you didn't like gardening."

"I don't see how that's insulting, Jane-Ann," Jackson said and took a sip of tea. "Those of you in the garden club have a special interest in *gardening*, at least most of you do. Jessica does not. I'm sure she enjoys seeing the beautiful gardens and the flowers, but has no interest in seeding, nurturing, and pruning to achieve them. One can have an appreciation for something without having a great interest in active participation. This flower show is also a social event she thought you would enjoy. And, think of how wonderful it will feel to tell your friends that you were at a social engagement with *Her Majesty*, along with celebrities. Why your friends will be as green as their plants when you tell them."

That mollified her and we finished our breakfast in silence, until my aunt asked, "What are your plans today, Jackson?"

"Museums, Jane-Ann and I'd better get going, too, if I want to beat tourists to Victoria & Albert this morning."

"Would you like for Mr. Herren to drive you? Elsie has her car and driver."

"No but thank you. I'll take a taxi and then go from there. I'd prefer to walk in that part of the city. The Tube is always somewhere nearby if I want to venture farther afield."

"Ask Mr. Herren to arrange the taxi for you."

"Thank you, I will." Just as he reached the door, he turned and said, "Have a wonderful time…the both of you."

***

"Lady Toddle," Mr. Herren announced.

Elsie Blake Tattersdown had been my dearest friend in university and she'd been my flatmate when I met Will. Her husband Alexander had been one of my husband's friends. Elsie's parents had once owned a large dairy farm, which she was glad to see the back of, mainly because rumor had it that she'd been named for the family's first cow. Today, my attractive brunette friend was wearing a sky-blue, cotton dress that brought out the color of her eyes, and those eyes were sparkling with mischief. She'd heard all about my aunt.

"Don't get up," she said, taking a seat next to my aunt on the brick-red sofa in the morning room. "You must be Carola's aunt."

"Yes, this is Jane-Ann Simmons," I said, providing a very informal introduction.

"How d' you do? Looking forward to today?" Elsie asked.

"My yes. I've just learned it's a special day."

"Oh, indeed it is. Lots of press, and that can be a bore, but the gardens are fresh and the weather today is gorgeous. You look very nice, Mrs. Simmons."

My aunt was wearing a lavender cardigan over a white blouse and floral skirt. On her feet were her sensible walking shoes. I'd told her this was not a 'fashion footwear' event. "I hope it won't be too difficult getting around," she said. "I've got my cane, but if Queen Elizabeth can manage it, so can I. She's a good deal older than I am."

"Good for you," Elsie cheered. "That's the spirit. We should start out. The car is waiting. I trust you enjoyed a hearty breakfast. There will be places to rest at the show and we will take tea there later. It can be a full day out, though."

"Well, ummm, yes, Lady Toddle, whatever you suggest," my aunt stuttered.

"Please, call me Elsie. I've heard so much about you that I feel I've known you for years."

Aunt Jane-Ann simpered. "Oh, why, thank you…Elsie."

Chapter Four

We arrived at The Chelsea Flower Show shortly after ten. Elsie's driver got us as close to the entrance as he possibly could, but there was still a little walk. I worried that my aunt would not have the stamina to tour the entire show, but she marched on ahead of us, excited as a young girl. Elsie and I had to walk quickly to catch up.

"Is that the woman who starred in *As Time Goes By*?" Aunt Jane-Ann asked, referring to Dame Judi Dench. Now, I *knew* my aunt was a PBS junkie. That sitcom ran for years beginning in the early '90s and into the early 2000s but was apparently still being shown in reruns on her Channel 13.

"Yes, I believe so," I said, as we strolled along.

"Oh, my word. I can't believe it. Would it be rude to..."

"YES," Elsie and I said in unison, without waiting for the rest of her question.

"Do either of you know her?"

"I've met her," Elsie replied. "She's very nice, but let's allow her some peace to enjoy the gardens, shall we. You're likely to see a number of celebrities, but, as a rule, we do not approach them unless they address us or one of us knows them well enough. A nod in passing or a 'good morning' or 'good afternoon' is sufficient. As for any member of the Royal Family, you should not approach *them*. If they wish to speak with you, it will be made known."

"I'm representing the *Hilly Dale Gazette* from my home state of Arkansas, Elsie. Would you allow me to interview you and have your photo taken for our local paper? You are a viscountess, and everyone in Hilly Dale already knows about Jessica, I mean, Carola. You'll be a new interest for them."

Elsie looked at me and then back at my aunt. "I'd be delighted, Jane-Ann. We shall pick your favorite garden and there you can interview me and we'll have a photo. Will that suit?"

"Oh yes, thank you!"

Aunt Jane-Ann goggled at the photographers, as well as the press conducting interviews with celebrities, as we made our way down the wide path lined with booths. I was happy that Elsie had agreed to an interview which meant with any luck my aunt would not approach anyone else.

"We'll stop at The Great Pavilion where you will see..." Elsie began, but stopped abruptly when a smartly-dressed woman with a glossy black bob and wearing a red dress, stepped into our path.

"You're Jessica Keasden, or, should I say, Carola, Duchess of Hearthe."

God, it was Isabel Allensworth, the gossip columnist who had 'outed' my identity two years ago. She was a close friend of Cecilia's mother, the one I suspected had instigated the 'outing.'

"Ms. Allensworth," I acknowledged.

"What's going on with your writing, Duchess? Nothing new in a while. Have you abandoned it since you're back in England? Have you left all your fans in the lurch now that you have a new love interest spending time with you at Lilac House? How does the family feel about that?"

Ignore, ignore, ignore, but it was so difficult with this woman. "I've not abandoned my writing at all. The third in the *Secrets of Snowdonia* series is coming out the end of next month and I'm starting work on a new *Harriet Donovan*, but I'm here to enjoy the gardens. Please excuse me."

I'd just turned my back on her when I heard her call out, "Is your *step*-daughter-in-law joining you here. I'd love to get an interview with the *new* Duchess of Hearthe."

I turned around, smiled, and said, "Perhaps you should take that up with her *mother*. I understand you're quite good friends." And with that I took my aunt's arm, and with Elsie in tow, walked swiftly away.

"Oh, Carola, should you have antagonized Isabel? And how did she know about you and Beck at Lilac House?"

"I'm sure you can guess."

"Simply dreadful woman. I remember what she did to you."

"What was that?" my aunt asked.

"You remember when all that came out about Hilly Dale and me being called 'The Duchess of Hillbilly Dale?' You and others were quite offended because you thought I'd said that."

My aunt nodded. "Unfortunate," she said. "You really shouldn't have said such a thing."

"As I said then, *I* never said it. *That* was the woman who broke the news. Don't turn around and look. She's expecting that. She wants a reaction. I gave her a small one."

"I declare, what a nasty person," Aunt Jane-Ann cried. "Spreading rumors. Now, where are the gardens? I came to see the beautiful gardens, not a busybody."

"Let's take a stroll down the garden path and have a look," I said.

We all had our favorites. I loved the 'Welcome to Yorkshire' garden with its small rock 'house" and canal. My aunt was fascinated by the 'Back to Nature' garden the Duchess of Cambridge designed, particularly the rope swing and tree house. "So clever, she is" she commented. "Her own children will love this."

"It was near the 'Back to Nature' garden that my aunt interviewed Elsie while I surreptitiously videoed the exchange and then took photos of them. Elsie favored the 'Art of the Viking' probably because she spent part of her honeymoon in Scandinavia visiting Alexander's relatives, although lovely as it was, I was unsure why this garden evoked pleasant memories for her. She detested his relatives.

Aunt Jane-Ann finally admitted she needed a rest. Elsie suggested a tea room on the premises. We were fortunate enough to find a small table where we sat for a half-hour talking about what we'd seen and what else was left. The commotion outside started just as we'd exited and were heading toward yet another garden. It was clear from the excitement around us that Her Majesty had arrived. After walking over to stand where a group was gathering, trying to appear uninterested, but failing somewhat, my eager aunt pushed to the front, saying that she was a member of the press. Murmuring apologies to those we passed, Elsie and I hurried to make sure she wasn't going to attempt a meeting with the queen.

"I see her," Aunt Jane-Ann said, completely awestruck. "She's just yards away talking to that man."

"The president of the RHS," Elsie murmured.

"Oh do you know him?"

"We've both been introduced to him, Aunt."

"My Heavens. The *president.* Is it all right to take a quick photo of them?" she asked, taking out her phone. Yes, my aunt had purchased a smartphone for the trip, and Jackson had taught her how to use it.

"I wouldn't," I said, thinking she might show Gatsby Gregson and Peter Franklin the pictures and they would try to appropriate them and sell them. With a sigh of resignation, she dropped her phone back into the small handbag I loaned her. She could not take that huge tote she carried into The Chelsea Flower Show.

"But why isn't she wearing a hat, Jessica, and she's not wearing her usual bright colors. She's wearing a light-green coat. I can barely see her dress underneath, but, oh, my. The Queen!" My aunt gasped. "The Queen!"

"I really couldn't say about her attire. This isn't an engagement that requires a hat, and she does have an extensive wardrobe."

"Perhaps she didn't want to compete with the flowers," Elsie suggested. "Why don't we move on now?"

"She's wearing a floral dress! I can see under the coat now," my aunt cried.

"We should be moving along and not staring at her. It's rather impolite, Aunt."

"I haven't gotten a good look at those others who are with her," my aunt complained. "I don't see the Duchess of Cambridge." She paused and looked around. "Oh, there she is, and there's Prince William! Oh my goodness! What a handsome couple they are. Such class and elegance." Wait until I tell everyone! I don't know the others are with them."

"Some are security, but we will tell you who the others are later," I said, taking her arm while Elsie and I exchanged relieved looks behind my aunt's back. "We've still a couple of other gardens to see. Let's leave Her Majesty and Their Royal Highnesses to enjoy the gardens."

***

"How did it go with Jane-Ann today?" Jackson asked over a roast chicken dinner that night in the informal dining room, which, to be honest, was formal by most people's standards. Its square-paneled walls were painted white and a sparkling crystal chandelier bounced light off a pair of gilded mirrors that had been purchased from a European palace somewhere. Frankly, there were so many antique treasures in our houses that I barely remembered where many originated, especially here, since it was filled with things that had either been purchased somewhere or brought from Fielding House during the one-hundred-fifty-two years we'd owned this townhouse.

I groaned. "I'm glad she wanted a tray in her room and have an early night, but it went well, and Elsie was a blessing. Aunt Jane-Ann was quite the trooper all day. Unfortunately, the walking, the joy of seeing the gardens, and a brief sighting of Her Majesty and the Duke and Duchess of Cambridge proved to be a bit much for her."

"She's pretty remarkable. Did she squeal when she saw Her Majesty?"

"No, thank goodness, but she did when she saw Judi Dench standing a few feet from us."

"Please tell me she didn't make a fool out of herself in front of that great actress."

"No. Let's just say, in honor of The Chelsea Flower Show, Elsie and I nipped it in the bud. There was no asking for autographs or photographs, even when she saw an actor from *Downton Abbey* near The Great Pavilion. She wanted to follow him inside, but we steered her away. We'd already been through it and she saw him on the way out. We did allow her to take pictures of the gardens and we took photos of her and with her, so she will have plenty to talk about with her garden club. Perhaps there will be a picture of her in the news, so she'll have that too. The press was everywhere. Elsie allowed Aunt Jane-Ann to interview her for the *Hilly Dale Gazette* and she even posed for pictures. How was your day?"

"Wonderful. The V&A is just as I remembered it. And after that I took a tour of the Tower of London. Oddly, I'd never been."

"What did you think of it?"

"To be honest, I didn't take the real tour. I already knew all the history, of course, and went to the places I wanted to see, so I managed to get through the whole thing in under two hours, but it was intriguing to think of all those people who lived and died there. I wasn't fond of seeing The Gherkin nearby, but I suppose the juxtaposition of the ancient and modern was *something* to behold and made a striking photograph. I took a lot of pictures and bought a couple of trinkets in the gift shop. After that, I came back here and had a rest, and now I'm enjoying a delicious meal in the company of a dear friend."

My phone pinged. "Oh, it's Beck. He's checking to see how the day went. Excuse me a moment." Despite having a rule of no phones at the dinner table, I typed a very short message because I knew Beck was concerned, knowing my aunt as he did.

How was it? he texted.
It went well. Your day?
Long. Have a good time in Cornwall, he answered.
Wish you could join us.
So do I. Too far for short stay.
See you at Fielding House?
Plan to arrive the following Friday. Love you.
Love you, too.

"I apologize. Beck and I try to stay in touch every day, either by phone or text, depending on what's going on in our lives."

"I know you said there were no plans for marriage, but are you certain about that?"

"It's still new, Jackson. He joins me at Lilac House most weekends. It's a nice break for him from London, and it's not *too* far a drive after he leaves work. It gives me time to focus on my writing, and visit my children during the week, if I choose. We aren't rushing into anything. He's adjusting to his job and life here, and there's Jordan to consider. I know he is happy to be near her."

"Where is it she's going to school again?"

"Bristol."

"And I believe you mentioned once that she's dating Liam. That's a *hoot.* Can you imagine the gossip about you and Beckham if they married?"

"Yes," I stated emphatically. "They are very happy together. Aisling's delighted. I'm thankful *she's* dating James Walkstone. He isn't like some of Liam's friends. The one she dated shortly before she moved to Hilly Dale with me was a known cad, bouncing from girl to girl. Aisling is pretty serious with James now. They met at Alistair's wedding, if you'll remember. He's graduating from St. Andrews this term. Already has a job lined up, I understand."

"From a good family?"

"He's the Earl of Cradleburn's youngest son. His father is a friend of mine...and was of Will's. You met the earl at the wedding. His wife died early last year. Skiing accident in Austria while they were on holiday."

"Terrible! I remember him. Interesting fellow. Excellent lineage. Were you close friends with his wife?"

"I wouldn't say close like Elsie, but we were friendly. The countess and I met years ago when our daughters were in school in Switzerland. Dessie went on to finish there, but, as you know, I brought Aisling home after Will died. She wasn't happy at the school, but she developed excellent language skills in that couple of years."

"She's like you in a way. You picked up your English accent quickly, I imagine. Speaking of language skills, the college board of directors finally forced Tim Hayes to fire Patrizia di Santi."

"Is that so?" Ms. di Santi was the International Students Coordinator who, according to my daughter, was useless.

"I believe it was either that or he was going to lose his job," Jackson shared before taking a bite of his roast chicken. "You know, I shouldn't gossip, but Tim had to confess to his wife that he'd had an affair with Patrizia before the useless twit told her herself."

"I'm certain that rocked Hilly Dale Methodist." Tim's wife was the minister there.

"Oh, it did. She's still with him, but I understand it's not going well. She is terribly embarrassed, especially because she does premarital and marital counseling. Tim's been groveling, and his wife has been struggling with 'forgive and forget.' The 'forgive' is easier than the 'forget,' I imagine."

"What happened to Ms. di Santi?"

"She got a hostess job in a restaurant on the East Coast."

"You're joking! I know Aisling said she shouldn't have been in that position at the college, but surely she could have gotten another job in education."

"I don't think she wanted one. Her main goal was to find a husband. Hopefully, the next time she does, it won't be someone else's."

"Oh, Jackson, I miss our chats. There's not much to talk about here. At Lilac House, unless Beck's there, I'm working, and at Fielding House, things have changed since Cecilia is the mistress. I stay only a few days. I come to London on occasion to visit Beck, take care of business, or socialize with friends. Elsie and some others keep me up-to-date on our set, but it's fun to talk about things in Hilly Dale. Thankfully, though, I'm no longer 'news,' there, and it never was a bother here. There's too much else going on, and too many others with more interesting tales to tell."

"So, has Cecilia's mother been playing nice?"

"I don't know, but I think she's become frustrated. No one's paying her much mind, and Cecilia isn't doing a lot in the way of charity work, estate support, event-planning, or involving herself in Hearthestone Vale and the surrounding villages. Any of that would help raise her profile. I understand Damaris is trying to get a reality show started again, but this time about wives and girlfriends of the nobility. *That* is not going over well. She's had no takers, at least no one I know would be on something like that."

"*She's* not even a member of the nobility," Jackson said, and burst into laughter. "She's a wannabe."

"True, but she wants Cecilia involved. I know Alistair won't want that at all. If he has to, he'll involve the family legal team. To tell you the truth, Cecilia isn't, well, she's just not what I expected."

"How so?"

"It's hard to say. Maybe she isn't adjusting to her new role. I know it's difficult to grasp all the rules and the ins-and-outs of things, but she knew what she was getting into. They dated for several years."

"Hmmmm. I can see it taking some time. One can imagine what it would be like to be married to a duke, but I'm certain the reality is different. On another subject, when we get to Cornwall, I'd like to visit a couple of places by myself. Will that be a problem?"

"Of course not, but why?"

"I'd like to visit Bath, and it's a drive from where we'll be staying. I thought I go for a day or so. You need family time with Jane-Ann, and, frankly, I need a break from her. If she wasn't sleeping and snoring on the way over, she was going on about how it was time she'd gotten an invitation and how disgusted she was that you had chosen to give up your American citizenship completely. It was a small thrill seeing her reaction to this house and hearing you referred to as 'Your Grace.'"

"I explained to her when I renounced my citizenship the reason why. It made a lot more sense, personally and financially. My life is here."

"I hope she's been suitably impressed by it. She's been given a private tour of London by hired car. She's met a viscountess, visited the world-famous flower show with the queen and other senior members of the royal family in attendance, and seen celebrities, not to mention she's staying in a very expensive area of the city in a townhouse owned by a duke, and she's only been in England two and-a-half days!"

"Don't forget that she flew on a private jet."

"Oh, yes. I remember her telling Gatsby Gregson that you did that all the time. Now, she can say it's true *and* that you and she 'hobnobbed' with royalty."

"She didn't know the others but that's all right, believe me. I was planning to take her to lunch tomorrow and then a bit more sightseeing. Would you like to join us?"

"Thank you, but no. I believe I'll take in Westminster Abbey. You're not taking her there are you?"

We were silent for a few minutes, enjoying the chicken and vegetables. I was thinking about tomorrow and where I'd take my aunt that wouldn't be difficult. Harrod's maybe. We could spend at least a half-day there, and with plenty of places to eat, it seemed ideal. I sincerely hoped she didn't want to tour The Tower of London just to view the crown jewels. I wanted her to rest for The Eden Project after all the walking she did at the flower show.

"Jessica? Are you listening?"

"What? Oh, I'm sorry. I was thinking of somewhere to take Aunt Jane-Ann tomorrow. I've settled on Harrod's. Shopping and lunch, perhaps tea, should be fine."

"I'm sure it will be. I was saying that I know you haven't asked, but there's news of Heather James. Your aunt and I discussed whether we should tell you."

I raised my hands to my face and peered between my fingers. "Is she dead?" I asked, immediately thinking of her mental state when I'd left. She'd been placed into psychiatric care in Little Rock after she'd pushed her lover John Knoss off a bridge and into Dagnabbit Creek February of 2017. If Beck and I hadn't been nearby to see him floating by, he would have died of hypothermia. After that, Heather completely cracked and threatened Beck's ex-wife who was John's lover, with a knife.

It was due to the fall-out that I became not just Jessica Keasden, my *nom de plume*, but Carola, Duchess of Hearthe to people everywhere, but the ones who mattered were in Hilly Dale, Arkansas. My private relationship with Beck was exposed and became fodder for gossip. Aunt Jane-Ann had been both mortified and delighted that she'd been thrust into the spotlight.

"Is she dead?" I asked again.

"No, she isn't dead. You can take your hands down."

"Thank goodness for that," I replied with relief. Heather had been a good friend…once, but she used me after I returned to Hilly Dale. She used several people in order to exact revenge on three of her high school classmates known as 'The Three B's' - Beck, Bianca, and Betsy. Heather became a crazed Jessica Keasden fan, too, when my 'real life' was revealed. Trying to ruin my career, under a screen name she had posted ugly comments on my author sites. "What's happening?" I finally asked.

"They may be releasing her. She's been in treatment for over two years. According to all accounts, she is remorseful. Her psychiatrist believes she didn't intend to kill John with her stupid antics on the bridge. She was drunk when she attacked Bianca, so she's been in rehab for that. She's done very well in therapy and treatment. Apparently, a judge agreed. She can leave the psychiatric facility.

There's no jail time, as neither John nor Bianca pressed charges and both have left the state, but Heather will be monitored for some time. The kicker is she cannot return to Hilly Dale. There was a petition presented that the majority of citizens signed."

"Run out of her only home," I said softly, and shook my head. "Where will she go? One son is in prison, and her daughter graduated from high school almost two years ago. She was so proud of her the night she was in the Homecoming Court, Jackson. I don't know about her other son. He was in university while I was in Hilly Dale. What will they do?"

"The son not in prison moved to Oregon right out of university. Krista got a scholarship to the University of Alabama, so that's where she is now. Her father Steve Taylor and his wife are very supportive of her. As for Heather, I believe she's going to live with an aunt in Little Rock. She has to continue regularly seeing a psychiatrist for a number of years."

"What a sad situation. I wish I could have helped her."

"She was so warped with misplaced jealousy, and stuck in the past, that I don't think you could. When you put it together with alcohol, it's not a good mix. You and Beck getting together may have pushed her over the edge, but there was nothing you could do. You didn't know anything about her when you moved to Arkansas. Now, let's move on and focus on this wonderful food. May I pour you another glass of wine, Your Grace?"

Chapter Five

At 7:00 a.m., Jackson, Aunt Jane-Ann, and I set off for Cornwall, with me driving. The journey from London to Trevenston Manor near Port Tristan normally took around six hours including a short stop. Naturally, one would think that with traveling companions the trip would seem faster, but when one of those travelers was my Aunt Jane-Ann who alternated between sleeping, complaining, stressing about driving on the 'wrong side of the road,' and comparing everything to America, and the other traveler imparted the history of various towns we passed, it became more and more difficult for me to control my increasing crankiness. At least Jackson was able to share some of the driving duties after we got out of London, which was the one thing that made the trip bearable at the moment.

The *only* thing Aunt Jane-Ann didn't complain about were the motorway service stations. She declared most of them superior to the rest stops in America. Jackson and I thought so too. With their places to get petrol – gas I had to call it with my aunt - shop, eat, rest, and use the facilities, and spend the night if necessary, they made the journey a bit more tolerable. We stopped more than a couple of times just so she could look around and take photos at the nicer ones.

While Jackson was using the facilities and grabbing some coffee, Aunt Jane-and I took another opportunity to stretch our legs in a green space. "Look at that!" my aunt cried and excitedly took a picture of a sign depicting a squatting dog with the words 'Please, No Dog Fouling' printed above. "Do you think a shop will have that sign for sale? I'd like one for my yard. Margo Hunter's two Pekinese dogs crap on my front lawn every time she walks them. She does *nothing* about it. Oh, she does if I'm on the front porch, but I've watched her from the window. She doesn't pick that mess up unless she sees me. Let them crap in their own yard!"

After we got in the car, I told Jackson, whose turn it was at the wheel, what we'd seen. He laughed so hard he nearly missed the exit.

"Don't you have the fence, Aunt Jane-Ann?"

"No, I took that monstrosity down. It was unfriendly. Everyone said so, but at least it kept crapping dogs off the property!"

Oh my!

***

Nine hours after we'd begun the journey to Cornwall, we reached the cut-off that would take us to Trevenston Manor. A sign at the crossroads pointed south for Port Tristan, which was not far from Aunt Jane-Ann's *Doc Martin* territory. Port Tristan began as a small fishing village but had grown larger and now catered to tourists.

Much had been made of the general area thanks to the popularization of that television series, but mainly it was the Arthurian myths and legends shaped by Geoffrey Monmouth in the twelfth-century that brought a hoard of visitors each year to our area, specifically to the village of Tintagel. The fact that the castle, now in ruins, was built by the first Earl of Cornwall in the thirteenth century, did nothing to dispel the legends. Archaeological evidence of a much earlier civilization on what was known as Tintagel Island lent credence to the British cleric Monmouth's works.

Will and I had visited Tintagel and climbed up the side of a cliff to view the ruins not long after we married. I mentioned that as I drove up the narrow, rural road to the Fielding-Smythe cliff-top property.

"I'm looking forward to seeing it," Jackson declared. "I've been walking every day for two months to get in shape for the climb."

The climb hadn't been so difficult when I was in my twenties, but now that I was approaching fifty and Jackson already in his sixties, the trek up the cliff would most likely be arduous this time round; however, it was one of his goals, so we would at least try.

"I'll pass on that," Aunt Jane-Ann said. "There are scenes of Cornish cliffs on *Doc Martin*. I don't want to fall into the sea trying to scale one."

This was a good thing, because she had not been invited on this sightseeing expedition.

It had begun to rain when I reached the entrance to Trevenston Manor. Driving between the two gray pillars, with their dull iron gates

39

standing open, I followed the lane, dreading what was about to appear. It was fitting that my first glimpse, in over six years, of the eighteenth-century, gray stone, three-story house waiting for me in the distance was through a downpour. I slowed the car without even realizing it. I'd never liked the rectangular house with its many windows and double-flight of stairs leading to the main entrance. To me, the house seemed stark. Except for the stunning views of the sea and cliffs, I found it dreary and lonely, now even more so since Will had died at sea a few miles away.

Because I'd agreed to Cornwall, I planned the trip to The Eden Project to have time away from the house, but I knew I had to face my fears and my memories at some point.

"Are we supposed to walk to the house?" Aunt Jane-Ann snapped. "In the rain?"

"Sorry," I said, stepping on the accelerator.

"We're not climbing all those steps, are we?" she asked when we reached the house.

"No." Turning the car to the right, I drove under a porte-corchère on the north side of the house, honked the horn, turned off the engine, and got out of the car. "Do you need any help Aunt Jane-Ann? There will be some steps to reach the main floor."

"I'm stiff from sitting in the car the last two hours, but I'll make it. How about you, Jackson. You're not getting any younger."

"Jane-Ann, you always know the perfect thing to say at just the right time."

When I opened the door to the house, there on the other side stood a surprised-looking Mr. Euston, the property's caretaker. He ran his fingers through his salt-and-pepper hair and then adjusted his dark jacket.

"Good afternoon," I said, "Or is it early evening, by now." With the darkening sky and the exceedingly-long trip it *felt* like it should be midnight.

"Your Grace! I apologize. I had no idea you had arrived. I was just coming to turn on the light in the porte-corchère for you." He flipped a switch and the large, black, electric coach house lanterns on either side of the exterior door came on.

"I should be the one to apologize, Mr. Euston. I fully intended to ring you when we reached Cornwall, but the weather turned a bit nasty and I forgot."

"Perfectly understandable. I must admit I was getting worried." Mr. Euston, a life-long resident of the Port Tristan area, hid his Cornish accent for some reason in my presence. He was quite formal, more so than Mr. Herren, or Mr. Bailing at Fielding House. I introduced my aunt and Jackson before we took the short flight of stairs to the main floor.

Following Mr. Euston, we passed through a door and entered the surprisingly small foyer with its slate floors and cream walls. It hadn't changed since I was last here. There was the same polished mahogany table pushed against a wall with a stormy seascape in a simple wood frame above, and before us was a mahogany, curving staircase with no carpet runner. You would have thought with the chandelier switched on, as well as a table lamp, the foyer would have been welcoming and brighter, but it was drab to me.

"Not quite what I expected from such a grand exterior," commented Aunt Jane-Ann. "Small."

I ignored her, but she was correct. The first time I'd visited, I'd been disappointed. The interior was nothing like the elegance of the townhouse or the Elizabethan opulence of Fielding House.

"All the rooms are ready, Your Grace. Yours is, of course, the one you have always used. Dr. Barker and Mrs. Simmons are down the hall. I will let Mrs. Euston know you've arrived. She's preparing a nice dinner."

"The rooms are on the next floor," I told my traveling companions.

"Are we to be in the attic," my aunt complained. "All these stairs."

"Thank you, Mr. Euston. I'll show them their rooms. Our bags are in the car. After he left I turned to my aunt, "I'm sorry that there are so many stairs. This house does not have an elevator, but I'd appreciate it if you didn't complain in front of the staff. Where you came in is a lower, partial level of the house. It's where the kitchens are."

"So, this is really a four-story house," she stated firmly. "It looked to be three."

How nitpicking she could be!

"No. Consider the very lowest level a partial half-story, if you must. The attic is above where we'll be staying. It used to be the servants' quarters."

"You're getting gripey, Jessica. You need to eat something. When *is* dinner? I barely had anything at that last service station. You and Jackson ate nothing there."

"Jackson, you're awfully quiet," I said.

"Just taking in the place, and ready for a rest. I can see why Beckham couldn't come this weekend. Does it always take so long to arrive in Cornwall?"

"It is quite a ways, but to answer your question, no, it doesn't take this long." I glanced at my aunt. "Let me show you your rooms. I'm sorry you have to climb another flight, Aunt Jane-Ann, but there are no bedrooms on this floor. Jackson, would you please help her."

"I don't need any help," she snapped at me as we started up the staircase. "These stairs creak. You should have that man fix them." Not for the first time, did I see a resemblance to my mother-in-law, Josephine. She could be quite the nitpicker. Although she had mellowed in *her* later years, my aunt had not.

All the rooms to the sides and back had sea views. I almost asked to be placed in a room facing the front lawn, but that would have been me avoiding the inevitable. I already knew I'd have a corner room with a small balcony facing the sea, but I could still put off entering it for a little while longer.

Dinner was held in the small, slate-floored informal dining room on an oak table that had probably sat there since the house was built. The chairs were high-backed wood with rush seats and they were uncomfortable. We were all exhausted, fussy, and in no mood for a fancy set-up. Mrs. Euston served us roast pork, roasted potatoes and a medley of carrots and peas. The peas I picked out and pushed to the side of the plate.

Jackson looked at me and said, "You know, Jessica, this place has an odd feeling. I picked up on it immediately when we entered, and then again as we walked to our rooms. It's not exactly eerie and I don't sense ghosts, but…I don't know. Maybe I've read too many Daphne du Maurier novels and expect one of her characters to appear."

"She lived in Cornwall," my aunt, the former librarian informed us. "Her novels were moody. Perhaps that's what you're picking up on. I sense nothing."

This was one of the few times I'd ever heard my aunt mention anything about authors or their works, which I found strange for someone whose profession had been working with books, and who was a member of a book club.

"The views are spectacular though, "Jackson added. "I have a marvelous little stone balcony and even with the stormy weather, I enjoyed the view. I could just make out the waves hitting the rocks to the south, and the sound that made was relaxing. They were a little loud, of course, but the rhythm was the same. I look forward to some cliff walking while I'm here, if the weather's nice."

"Stay well back from the edges, Jackson," I warned.

"I remember what you said about cliff falls."

"We haven't had one…yet, and I hope we don't. Naturally, there has been a great deal of erosion. That's a given when you live near the sea. Storms are incredible at times."

"I hope to take a trip to the Bedruthan Steps, and go to Boscastle, and Tintagel like we have planned," Jackson said. "There's so much to see and learn in Cornwall. The history in itself is fascinating. Of course, I hope to get that trip to Bath planned, but I don't know if I will stay the night. Too much to see and do here, and we don't have a week to spend. I daresay this house is easier to get around in than at Fielding House."

"It has too many stairs," my aunt pointed out. "Stairs outside; stairs inside. You really do need an elevator here, Jessica."

"It's never been my decision and you simply can't alter a Grade 2 listed property anyway you choose or any time you choose. Besides, you have stated several times that you have stairs in your own house and use them,"

"Yes, I do, but those are *my* stairs. I know them. These are foreign ones, and they creak."

"So, Jane-Ann, how are you enjoying your trip to England?" Jackson asked, while cutting his roast pork.

"Well, I'll say this. The English take care of the elderly."

"What?" Jackson and I said in unison. "The OAP?"

"What's that?"

"Old Age Pensioners, Aunt."

"Whatever you call them, they are taken care of. When we were driving through a village on our way here, I saw an official street sign. On that sign were two people bent over walking; one had a cane. Do you know what that sign had on it?" Not waiting for an answer, she continued, "*Elderly People*. Did either of you see it?"

"No," we both said.

"One of us was probably driving and the other resting. It *was* a long drive, Jane-Ann." Jackson rolled his shoulders. Despite the numerous breaks and change in drivers, the trip had been tedious for obvious reasons.

"My favorite is still the one she wanted to buy about dogs pooping,"

"Jessica, talk of pooping is not dinner table conversation, even if it has to do with dogs, but let me tell you, Jackson, I need a sign like that because of Margo Hunter. I'm tired of having to remove crap from my front lawn."

Jackson was shaking with laughter. "Well, Jane-Ann, perhaps we will have to find you one of those signs or maybe the Hilly Dale print shop or sign-maker can custom one for you," he said. "On that note, I think it's time for me to retire with a good book. *Frenchman's Creek* I think. On a cursory walk through the house, I spied a nice selection of Du Maurier books in the small library. I noticed the books were autographed first editions. I'll be careful with them. Of course, she spent time in Cornwall, like Jane-Ann mentioned a few minutes ago. Boddinick and Fowey at first, but there were at least a couple of others. I'd like to go there. It stands to reason she might have known your family."

"Quite possibly. Enjoy your reading," I said, and after a moment, added. "You know, if you would like to stay here longer, you can always meet up with us at Fielding House a day or two later. I'm sure you could borrow a car here. The Euston's have their two, but we've always kept one for our use. You are welcome to drive it to Bath or anywhere else you would like. It won't be anything fancy. We don't keep cars like that here."

"An excellent suggestion. Thank you, Jessica. I'll think on it. There's so much I want to see, and I know," he added, glancing at my aunt, "that it might not be something Jane-Ann is interested in."

"Why? I'm here to see what Jessica's life is like and see her *chosen* country. I want to know what compelled her to give up her American citizenship."

My aunt switched from being personable to excited, to snappy, to rude, in minutes. I'd worry, except my mother once told me that she had always been like that.

"I could be wrong about this, Jane-Ann, but it might have something to do with her *children* having been born and raised here. They are English, and Jessica did spend more of her life in England than in America."

"I think I'll go on to bed," she announced. "It's been a long day. I hope I'll be able to sleep with the sound of the sea nearby, and creaking stair steps."

After she'd left, Jackson stood up, ready to go to his own room. "Her snoring would drown out the largest of waves pounding the cliff. I'm off to enjoy the sound – the sea, not her snoring. Her room is right next door, after all."

Chapter Six

Unable to avoid it any longer, I turned the blackened knob and pushed open the oak door, hearing its familiar squeak. My aunt was right. This *was* a creaky old house by the sea. The first thing to meet my eye in the white-washed room was a plain four-poster bed – the dark wood of unknown origin. A red-and-white quilt was carefully folded at the foot of the deep-green duvet. I stared at that quilt. It had been made for one of the old dukes by a local woman as a token of the village's thanks for opening Trevenston Manor during a violent storm that caused considerable damage to Port Tristan. Thankfully, no lives were lost due to the duke's generosity. It had been fortuitous that the family had even been in residence then, so seldom did anyone visit.

No lives lost. I wished fervently that had been the case during the sailing competition when Will died. For the moment, I was glad it was dark and the draperies drawn. That way I wouldn't have to look at the view from the window and French doors. The sound of the sea and this bedroom was enough to remind me of my loss. My earlier thought about switching rooms entered my mind again, and I almost bolted, but I had made the choice to come and face my demons.

After I showered and put on my pajamas, I removed the quilt, crawled into bed, and pulled up the duvet. The room would be chilly later after the fire in the stone fireplace grate burned itself out, and I'd probably be wishing for that quilt, but I couldn't bring myself to use it. I reached for my phone on the nightstand, leaned back on the fluffy white pillows and rang Beck to say goodnight.

"How's it going?" he asked.

"Fair to middling."

"Now, there's a Briticism."

"It's said in America."

"Not that often. So, is Aunt Jane-Ann behaving?"

"Better than expected, but she can be exhausting with her demands, complaints, and comments, and her fascination with British television programs knows no bounds."

"Because of you, I can see why the programs would attract her. Those in Hilly Dale who have never watched Masterpiece Theater or British comedies and dramas are probably glued to Channel 13 now, believing that's what kind of life you lead, and what it's like in the United Kingdom."

"She's at least watching some quality programs. The drive here was painfully slow, but there were some humorous moments." I told him about the 'No Dog Fouling' sign.

"I hope she has one made. That will set Hilly Dale on its ear, but the wording's a little formal for there. Making a sign that has the picture and the words 'Shit On Your Own Property' might be better."

"That would certainly make a statement."

"Or even more succinct, 'No shitting' with the picture of the squatting dog." Beck started laughing. "Or even..."

His laughter was contagious and I succumbed. When I managed to gain control, I begged, "Enough of your creativity. She took a photo that I'm sure she will post on her Facebook page."

"Jane-Ann has a Facebook page?"

"Oh yes. It's something new for her. Her friends are all on there, sharing photos, announcing club meetings, and posting their meals. I warned her not to do any of that while she's here. People probably already know she's not at home, but why remind them by posting pictures of her holiday. She's been advised not to post anything about me or my children. So far, she's been cooperating. I have told her she can post the photo of the three of us at The Chelsea Flower Show when she returns. Elsie doesn't mind."

"Are you all right at Trevenston? It's your first time back since..."

"It's strange. I'm in the same room I've always had. I almost bolted to the front of the house."

"But you didn't, and that's a step forward. Plans tomorrow?"

"Yes. I'm taking my aunt to The Eden Project."

"Good luck! Signing off. Love you."

"Love you too."

I felt a bit better after talking to Beck. Switching off the bedside lamp, I lay watching the dying fire cast shadows in the room and listening to the surf just a hundred yards away. There really was something about this house that disturbed me. It always had. Even Jackson had felt it, but he was right. It wasn't ghosts that haunted it. What I felt through this house was sadness. Was it because no one lived here? I mean, *truly* lived here.

The Euston's had an apartment on the top floor, but other than that, it had always been used as a holiday retreat for the Fielding-Smythes, and then only for a few weeks, if that. Anything could have happened here and we'd never know. *Had* something happened? An idea for my next *Harriet Donovan* began forming. What if someone in the town was keeping a secret? What if it involved the owners of the house?

I rolled over and punched the pillow next to me – the pillow on which Will used to sleep. Maybe it was time Alistair considered selling the house to a family who would love it and make it beautiful and full of laughter, driving the gloominess or whatever it was away.

I knew I'd slept a little when I was startled awake by someone heavily knocking on my door. Struggling out of bed, I threw on the bathrobe I'd dropped on the floor last night, and then tripped over the edge of the worn Turkish rug on my way to answer the continuous pounding. Bleary-eyed, I opened the door. Aunt Jane-Ann stood there, fully-dressed.

"Well, what are you still doing in bed? Don't country-folk rise early out here? I'm ready for my breakfast. Get up and get started, Jessica. I heard Jackson whistling as he went down the hall. He's probably waiting for his morning meal too."

"What time is it?" Jet-lag clearly had no effect on my aunt.

"It's nearly 7:00 a.m. Time to get up. It's going to be a glorious day. You have guests."

"Who?" I asked sleepily.

"Who? Me, for one and Jackson for the other."

"Right. Sorry. I'm not quite awake. Go to the room where we had dinner. I'll be down as soon as I wash and dress. The Eustons rise early."

"It's rude not to get up earlier than your guests. You should have been up an hour ago. If Beckham had joined us, I'd suspect you had been canoodling all night, but seeing as he's not here, you have no excuse, not that allowing him to sleep in the bed you shared with your late husband would have been the right thing to do."

Way to start my morning on a cheery note, Aunt Jane-Ann.

"Here," she said pushing past me into the room. "Let's get some light in here." She threw open the draperies covering the windows, one of which opened onto the small stone balcony. Stepping outside she called, "I've been out on my balcony already. Refreshing, Jessica. Clears the mind. Come out and take a few deep breaths." I heard her exaggerated inhale and exhale. Had the balcony been larger, would she have started jumping jacks?

I stepped over to a window. There it was. The Celtic Sea stretched into the distance in all her glory under a clear sky. White caps danced farther out on top of the blue water. No crashing waves today to remind me of what happened to Will. Turning, I looked at the quilt I'd placed on a chair. *No Lives Lost*. Not then. Picking it up, I returned the treasured gift to its rightful place at the foot of the bed.

"Hurry up, Jessica."

"I'll be down in a half-hour. Just let me dress, please."

Aunt Jane-Ann would have none of that. She informed me that she would wait on the balcony and enjoy the magnificent view. Since I'd refused to come to my room until the very last minute, I had not unpacked. Unzipping a hanging bag that I'd hung in the wardrobe, I took out dark-blue capri pants, a blue-and-white striped long-sleeved tee-shirt, and a long black cardigan. From the bottom of the bag, I extracted a pair of comfortable, black, low-heeled shoes. Following that, I opened my tote, grabbed underwear, and headed to the tiny bathroom – the only ensuite in the house.

After I'd showered, dressed, put on a little makeup and tied my hair in a ponytail, I felt more normal, despite not sleeping well. *A good strong cup of tea should fix that*, I thought as I walked into my room.

Aunt Jane-Ann had remained. Her back was to me and she was still admiring the view. I saw her glance at her watch. Before I said anything, I took in her attire to make sure it was suitable for today's adventure. She was wearing loose gray trousers, a white cotton blouse, and was carrying a navy jacket. On her feet were her black SAS lace-up walking shoes. The strap of her black crossbody bag was hanging over one shoulder and the bag itself was well past her hip. I'd have to show her how to wear that so she could be hands-free.

"I'm glad you listened about the layering. It's chilly this morning, but inside the Rainforest it will be..." I began.

"Don't dawdle, Jessica. You were always a dawdler." My aunt turned and looked at me just as she had when I was a child. "Get a move-on. Things to do today."

Aunt Jane-Ann had *clearly* had a restful night's sleep. Her blue-gray eyes were bright with excitement and she'd fluffed her gray hair more than usual.

"Do you want to join us today?" I asked Jackson during breakfast.

"Thank you, but no. I've decided it is the Bedruthan Steps today, and then a stop at Trerice to see the gardens and the manor. It's not that far. I noticed it listed in some of the brochures I picked up at the service station just as we entered Cornwall. Trerice was the home of the Arundell family, not to be confused by the Fitzalans of Arundel Castle in West Sussex, however." Jackson was ever the historian.

"We're off to The Eden Project if Jessica will finish her breakfast and stop dawdling."

"We shall have informative dinner conversations tonight," Jackson said, and stood up. "Mr. Euston has the car ready for me."

"Are you sure you're comfortable driving in Cornwall, Jackson?" I asked. "If not, I'm sure Mr. Euston can find a driver for you. There are some men in town who drive tourists here and there."

"No, I've got my bearings, and after driving yesterday, I'm comfortable with it. I'll see you at dinner tonight."

Chapter Seven

"I'm not sitting in a *wheelchair*. I'm not an invalid. I didn't do it at The Chelsea Flower Show and I'm not doing it at The Eden Project. I have my cane and I'm wearing my sensible walking shoes," my aunt announced after learning I'd reserved a chair for her.

"It's not a wheelchair. It's a motorized chair. This isn't like the flower show on Press Day," I informed her as we drove along. "It's not strolling around looking at the gardens, celebrities, and royalty, and having tea. While places are available to eat, there will be a lot more walking, temperature changes, and children running around."

"It's humiliating, that's what it is!" She gave a great sigh. "I suppose I see your point, however. Fine, but all photos and selfies must be done with me out of that chair and it out-of-sight, and I want no mention of this to Jackson. The last thing I need is for my friends to know that I was using one of those chairs!"

I kept my eyes on the road, but I could sense she was scowling at me. "Agreed," I replied. This would make it so much easier for the both of us.

"Jessica!" she cried a few minutes later. "There's a sign for Port Isaac! Turn NOW! I want to see where *Doc Martin* is filmed."

"I've tickets for The Eden Project today. As you can see, Port Isaac is not far from Trevenston Manor. We'll visit tomorrow, if you're up to it."

"Of course I'll be up to it. I have to get some photos of places I recognize."

"I promise you that we'll go."

Appeased, she was quiet for a while until she blurted, "I thought we were going to a garden, not some futuristic-looking place that reminds me of beehives. Is that The Eden Project? Are we early? Doesn't look like too many cars here yet."

It was 10:00 a.m., just thirty minutes after the opening. "Yes, we're here," I said, pulling into a parking lot. "Now, before we arrive at the entrance, let's decide what you want to see, and please don't say 'all of it,' Aunt." I handed her a copy of a guide to the project that Mrs. Euston had given me before we left.

Flipping through the booklet, my aunt declared she only wanted to see the Rainforest and the Mediterranean biomes. "I'm not interested in all of this conservation and ecological business. I'm here to see *flowers* and plants, and experience where they grow. I don't want to learn about energy, fuels, and crops. Just flowers and plants."

Just as well.

"I can't walk that far to the Visitor Center, Jessica, and I certainly don't want to ride on that *bus* I see over there."

Anticipating a complaint about taking a bus, I'd pre-arranged for a member of the Eden Project team to pick us up and take us to the Visitor Center at a specific time. We were a few minutes early, but I could see the man waiting for us a short distance away. Not only did he drive us to the entrance, he waited while our tickets were checked, and then escorted us to the appropriate person who could help with the motorized chair.

"Oh, yes, we have that," she said. "Carola Fielding-Smythe?"

"That's correct," I replied. Turning to the man who had brought us to the center, I said thank you and tried to offer him payment, but he refused.

"Of the Fielding-Smythes who own Trevenston Manor?" the young woman, blue eyes widening, inquired after the man left.

I nodded.

"I understand now why this was waiting at this location. You're…"

"Duchess of Hearthe," Aunt Jane-Ann volunteered. "And she's also the famous author Jessica Keasden." My aunt just couldn't stop 'helping.'

"Oh, I love your books! There are a couple of directors here today who might like to meet you. Perhaps even give you a personal tour."

"A personal tour? That would be wonderful." Aunt Jane-Ann cried, beaming.

I turned my head to avoid the young woman seeing my grimace. I really wanted to shush my aunt but it would have been rude to do so in front of the employee. Looking back at the staff member, I smiled and then said, "Thank you, but we'll be fine on our own. I'm sure the directors who are here have more important things to do today. Is the chair ready?"

Aunt Jane-Ann tried out her motorized chair and declared it fine. When we were out of everyone's earshot, she said, "She didn't call you, 'Your Grace.' And as for that dirty look you gave me – yes, I saw it - if you didn't want your title known, why did you use 'Carola Fielding-Smythe' when you arranged for this embarrassing chair."

"It's part of my name on my driving license, Aunt, and it's the name I go by."

"Oh, but we *could* have had a personal tour, Jessica, after she realized who you were."

When you announced it, I wanted to say.

"Why *didn't* you let her arrange that?"

"Because it's unnecessary and that would take up a director's time, and I'm sure the two here are attending to business matters. If they assigned us someone else, it would take away staff who should be assisting people who need actual help. You just needed a means of getting around. The place wouldn't have been shut down for us, and you would still use the chair. All a personal tour would do is draw attention, and from experience that makes it difficult to actually enjoy things. People stare, snap pictures, and some come up and want to talk."

"Well, in that case, let's get a move on. I think we should go straight for the Rainforest Biome," she directed. "It's the farthest one and one should always start there and work back, but before we do that, I want to use the restroom, and you should to, Jessica."

"I don't need to use it."

"Just try. We don't want to get stuck somewhere and one not be nearby."

"I'm certain they have restrooms throughout."

"Jessica, just go in there and *try*."

In a matter of minutes, I'd gone from a forty-nine-year-old duchess who could have gotten us a personal tour to six-year-old girl who needed to be encouraged to wee.

After exiting the restrooms, where I'd tried but failed, we started off down the path for the Biomes, passing through what could only be described as a travel through time. It began with prehistoric plants – the only thing my aunt found interesting. After that we hurried past the sensory gardens and eventually arrived at the entrance to the Biomes. The motorized chair could move fast with Aunt Jane-Ann at the controls. I found myself race-walking to keep up.

"See, there are restrooms here," I puffed, slightly out-of-breath.

"It never hurts to take advantage of them when you see one, and that last restroom was clean. This entire place, so far, has been extremely clean."

The Rainforest Biome temperature went from somewhat pleasant to tropical. It was somewhere in between that I took off my cardigan. After untucking my blouse, unbuttoning an extra button, and rolling-up the sleeves, I encouraged my aunt to do the same. She was fine with the jacket and rolling-up her sleeves, but when it came to the other, she was aghast.

"Untuck my blouse and undo an extra button! I don't think so, Jessica. That's not proper."

Good grief! It wasn't as if I asked her to strip to her underwear. "All right," I said in exasperation. "Be uncomfortable then. It may get steamy. If it hadn't been so cool out when we left I'd have worn shorts!"

"I don't understand this weather. We're near the coast, and it's May."

"We're farther north. You're not in Arkansas, but the humidity in the Rainforest will be worse than there, I imagine."

We followed the path, looking at the plants, marveling at the information, and stopping so my aunt could take pictures. "If that dome wasn't visible, I'd really believe I *was* in a rainforest."

"I agree, but at least we're able to leave it behind when we exit."

"I'd like to visit the Weather Maker exhibit. I wish I could take that canopy walkway," she remarked, looking at the guide, "and the cloud bridge looks interesting. Couldn't I leave the chair somewhere. It's such a nuisance. I want to cross that canopy walkway!"

Taking the guide from her, I looked over what she was reading. "I don't think that's a good idea, Aunt Jane-Ann. The walkway is narrow and you can't use the chair. With the cloud bridge there's a swirling mist, however, you could take the chair on that. This says the Weather Maker has rain and lightning exhibits, do you…"

"Fine," she snapped, but then the stubborn woman got up and headed for the narrow, wobbly, canopy rope walkway high above us. All I could do was hurry after her as she walked over to the entrance.

Not for the first time since we'd entered the Rainforest Biome had I thought this excursion was not the best idea I'd had. Sizing up the stairs to the top of the walkway, which was suspended between the two tallest trees in the place, my aunt turned back to me with a foolish look on her face. "Well, I suppose you're right. That is quite a climb."

It was on to the cloud bridge then, which was accessible for her chair, but upon return to where it had been abandoned, the chair had either been appropriated or removed. "You just can't trust anyone with things," Aunt Jane-Ann mumbled. "Can you get another one?"

"I doubt it. They don't have many and I had to reserve this last month."

"Fine! On to the cloud bridge. I can go up a ramp."

She could, but it was slow going. I was at least glad she'd brought her collapsible cane. Across the cloud bridge we went behind and ahead of families with children we had to dodge. As we walked across the bridge through the swirling mists, it really did feel like we were in the clouds. Children squealed in delight when they hit pockets of mist arising directly from the bridge. Aunt Jane-Ann was not quite as amused by this.

"Perhaps you were right, Jessica, and I should not have attempted this bridge. I shouldn't have abandoned the chair," she admitted, pulling a handkerchief from her crossbody bag. By the time she'd finished dabbing at her face, the white cotton was covered in her *Mirielle Marjolaine* foundation. Looking at the mess, she complained, "My makeup was supposed to be waterproof, and look at this. I'm a mess. When I return home, I'm taking this right back to that store in Fort Smith. It's not holding up to its claim. This place *is* more humid than Hilly Dale."

"Well, you've toured most of this biome, climbed up and down a pretty high ramp and have been to West Africa, tropical islands, and Malaysia, among other places. So, I'd say you have traveled quite a bit, so far." I reached over and smoothed what was left of her foundation back into place, so she didn't look blotchy. "They have a cooling room if you would like to go in there, or we can have a seat and rest for a little while."

"No, I'm ready to leave this place and cool off somewhere else. Let's stop and get something cold to drink, and maybe lunch before the Mediterranean Biome. I could use a rest, that's true."

So could I, but I was amazed by her fortitude. Finding a pleasant staff member, I explained about the motorized chair being left behind. "My aunt wanted to cross the canopy walkway, but then the stairs were going to be too much," I whispered. "I apologize and will be happy to pay any fee."

"That won't be necessary...Duchess," the man standing with the employee said. Startled, I turned to the man and recognized him as someone I'd met before at a charity event."

"Thank you. How kind of you, but I'm more than happy to pay. I'd hate for it to be damaged."

"Already taken care of," he said. "Joseph here has alerted someone to find the missing chair, haven't you?"

"Yes, I have, sir."

"I'm here on business and off to check on some things. Lovely to see you visiting The Eden Project."

After he and the employee left, my aunt piped up, "Well, why didn't you introduce me? I'm sure he's one of those directors, and he could have given us a tour."

"Aunt Jane-Ann, I didn't introduce you or even call him by name because I don't remember what it is. I believe I met him through Elsie at a charity event last year, but I can't be sure."

"It must be nice to have people know *you*, but you don't know them," my aunt sneered.

"Not especially. It can be embarrassing in some situations. As Jessica Keasden, it's not, mostly because no one expects an author to know all her fans, but as Duchess of Hearthe, it is. I should remember people, but I don't have a personal assistant to remind me."

"Well, he seemed to be a gentleman, and of the upper-class. Is he single?"

"If I don't even remember his name, how would I know his marital status? And I'm not looking for anyone. I'm with Beck."

"Yes, you are, but you could do much better. You were, after all, married to a duke. There are probably men lining up for you, even at your age."

There had been a couple interested before I left for Hilly Dale, but the pickings were slim. Most of the men with whom I was acquainted wanted much younger women as second or third wives.

"What are we waiting for, Jessica? Stop dawdling. Let's have lunch and go to the Mediterranean."

Though there were steps in the Mediterranean Biome, Aunt Jane-Ann fared much better, which meant so did I. All went well as we meandered along through the Mediterranean, part of Australia, and South Africa, until…

"California," Aunt Jane-Ann cried. "They have California? Why is it in a Mediterranean Biome."

"They're referring to the types of climates." Why she hadn't considered that South Africa and Australia were not in the Mediterranean basin either, I had no idea.

"But, *California*? I could have just taken a trip there and seen it for real."

***

"Did you enjoy your day of sightseeing?" I asked Jackson when we met for dinner that evening.

"Immensely. The Bedruthan steps, were, for want of a better word, amazing! I know they were formed by erosion, but I could imagine they once *were* a giant's stepping-stones. The scenery was breathtaking! Cornwall is mystical. I can certainly understand how myths and legends surround everything here."

"Cornwall does have some of the most beautiful and striking scenery," I agreed.

"I didn't venture to Du Maurier's home, but I went to Bodmin Moor and visited the *Jamaica Inn* and had lunch. I was disappointed in the rather theme-park atmosphere - signing and such - but the history! The *literary* history! The small museum! What did your mother think of Cornwall?"

"She loved it," I replied. "We came here each time she visited and drove all over the place. She enjoyed prowling through bookshops in every town we visited."

My mother had been an English literature professor. I'd done the Du Maurier tour, and in other parts of England had taken one for Jane Austen and another for Beatrix Potter. She'd balked at one for Shakespeare as she was one who had her doubts about who Shakespeare really was.

"Du Maurier was very popular when I was a librarian," Aunt Jane-Ann said. "I suppose I *should* take a tour of some of the places Evelyn went, but..." she stopped talking and looked at me across the table, "I'm not here *long* enough to do that and we're just visiting gardening exhibits, so my book club will be left without a program from my trip."

"You might have mentioned you wanted to see some places. I still might be able to fit one into..."

"Never mind, Jessica. It's always about you. You planned the trip." She took a bite of her salmon, declaring it delicious. "Mrs. Euston is an excellent cook. Plain, but excellent."

"Jane-Ann what did you think of today's journey?" Jackson asked.

"Extremely tiring. I'm surprised I'm able to have dinner tonight. I loved seeing Port Isaac! It was smaller than it appears on television, though."

Jackson furrowed his brow. "Port Isaac? I thought you went to The Eden Project."

"Oh we did," I replied, "but on the way back, Aunt Jane-Ann wanted to stop in Port Isaac. That's why we arrived home later than planned. She'd seen the sign on the way down. I told her we could go tomorrow as it isn't far from here, but she was so excited, how could I not acquiesce to her polite request." I smiled at my aunt.

Polite! What a fib. It had been more like a 'STOP NOW' demand. Why did she have to wake up just as we reached that particular place!

"Isn't that nice, but I was talking about The Eden Project."

"It was fine. The Rainforest was very warm and humid, nothing I couldn't experience standing in my back garden in Hilly Dale. I did find the inside waterfall beautiful, and there were some interesting plants and flowers. Jessica insisted I have a motorized chair, but I abandoned *that* soon enough. I wanted to cross the canopy walkway but couldn't – too many stairs. That's all I see in this country - stairs! We did go across the cloud bridge."

So much for not telling Jackson about the chair.

"I read about the place. They have ziplining. You could have done that, Jane-Ann."

I couldn't believe he said that with a straight face!

"I know what that is, but that's for young people. Apparently a *motorized* chair is for people my age. We had to take a land train back to the Visitor Center because Jessica couldn't get me another chair when mine disappeared."

"You got up and left it in the middle of a path to go to the canopy walkway. It was gone when we returned."

"You didn't try. That nice director would have gotten another one for me. You know, we *could* have had a personal tour by a director, but Jessica refused. I did enjoy the perfume garden in the Mediterranean Biome though. Being spring, the tulips were in bloom, too. I enjoyed that."

"You certainly took enough pictures for an outing that was merely fine," I said, stabbing a piece of salmon with my fork. Sometimes my aunt could sound so ungrateful.

"To show my friends. I wish you had been in more of them. They'll be so jealous I've been staying in *Doc Martin* country. We all watch that. Sometimes we have watch parties."

"I've never been invited to one of those, and I watch that series. Alas, we can't be invited to everything. We've all had a fascinating and tiring day, it seems," Jackson said. "I'm ready for bed."

Chapter Eight

Tintagel was on the agenda. It was Saturday, which meant more tourists. Originally, the trip was to be only Jackson and me but the previous night my aunt suddenly decided she wanted to go, despite the fact that we told her that it was an arduous trek up the side of the cliff. Aunt Jane-Ann must have been training for a marathon to prepare for this holiday because she showed little signs of slowing down.

"It has to do with Arthurian tales, Jessica. As a *librarian*, I would like to see something that has to do with legends and literature. As I said the other night at dinner, I must have something to discuss with my book club."

Apparently, the talk of Daphne du Maurier, Jackson's mention of literary history, and my late mother's interest in seeing various houses and locations, spurred her desire to visit the ruins of Tintagel Castle. However, a climb to the ruins to see the rumored location of King Arthur's conception, and in some circles, birth, was not happening for her. She physically couldn't do it.

After showing her some pictures online, she admitted that we were correct and thought a visit to Tintagel Village would suffice. There was plenty to see in the village but knowing my aunt's often brash ways and her demands, I didn't want any trouble. It wasn't like Jackson and I could rush from the ruins to her assistance.

It was decided that Aunt Jane-Ann would wait in the Camelot Castle Hotel, a large building that resembled a castle, but wasn't one. When my aunt began to argue that she would wait in the town of Tintagel, I mentioned the 'castle' had been featured on an episode or two of *Doc Martin* and that sealed the deal.

Camelot Castle was an impressive sight to see as we drove toward it. The structure had been built in 1894 and later turned into a hotel, capitalizing on the legend of King Arthur. Jackson and I escorted my aunt inside. While he took her to look at the view, I spoke to the manager, and using my title, which I rarely did, secured a special attendant for my aunt while she waited. The Fielding-Smythe name and the mention of Trevenston Manor went a long way in this part of Cornwall. Of course, I paid handsomely for the service, but it was worth it. She would be given anything she wanted, and if that included a walk along the cliffs, coffee, tea, a snack, a meal, or a private room, so be it.

"This is Mrs. Simmons," I said to the woman with honey-blonde hair and black spectacles who would be my aunt's companion. At least she wasn't a teenager. She looked to be in her late thirties. "Whatever she wants, within reason, please see that she gets it."

"Yes, Your Grace," the woman replied in a southern American accent with just a trace of an English one.

"Thank you."

"Dr. Barker?" The woman looked at Jackson. "Dr. Barker? It's me, Jeanie Bean. Everyone called me Jeanie Beanie Baby? It was while you taught in Virginia. I'm Jeanie Penhaligan now."

"Good Lord!" Jackson exclaimed. "That's been ages. I do remember you. Your interest was in Medieval."

"And here I am. Working in King Arthur country. Living the dream. Well, not exactly. I'm working here at Camelot Castle Hotel and living in Bude, but close enough. My husband works at a pub in Tintagel."

"Good for you," Jackson replied. "You are where you want to be. These are my dear friends, Jeanie." Turning to Jane-Ann, he continued, "You'll be in good hands. I remember Jeanie. She was one of my best students."

As Jackson and I walked away, I heard my aunt say, "I don't need a babysitter, but I'm glad you're American. I can understand you very well. Which way to see the ruins, Jeanie?"

"You can see them from outside, but there's not a way to reach them from here, Mrs. Simmons. Let me show you where the ruins are though."

"Poor thing," Jackson said as we got back in the car and drove to a parking lot near the town. "She was so intelligent and now she's babysitting your aunt and her husband works in a pub."

"She's where she wants to be, just like you said."

"I do want to see some of the village after the climb. I suppose we'll have to get Jane-Ann first."

"Yes, we will."

"Could you have arranged an overnight at the hotel for her?"

I wasn't sure if he was teasing or not, and I was afraid to answer him. We stopped in the Visitor Center before clomping down the long steep hill and walking along another pathway and then up where we stopped to view Merlin's Cave which was located across from us and below the ruins on Tintagel Island.

"Did you know that this is where Arthur was supposedly carried by waves and Merlin found him?" Jackson said.

"*Idylls of the King*," I replied. "Tennyson did a lot for the legend."

"Do you feel up to this?" he asked quietly. "It's getting windy."

"Yes," I said firmly, closing my eyes and listening to the sound of the waves crashing against the rocks, and trying not to remember how my husband was thrust by them against a cliff farther north. "I do. I have to."

"Let's go, then."

"Lead the way."

"I say let's get one of those Land Rovers on the way up when we get back to the tall hill. Easy going down but it will be more than a stretch of the legs to go up it, especially after this," he said, looking at the many steps going up the side of the cliff.

"I agree. I managed when I was in my twenties, but I still had to stop halfway and rest on one of those benches they have."

***

With a queue of people in front of and behind us, and some descending, we had to keep going. There was no turning round. When we finally reached the top, Jackson and I had to sit down on a rock wall for a few minutes to catch our breath, before getting up. I shivered in the cool wind. Wandering around, I found myself alone gazing through stone archway. In that moment, I felt at peace with my surroundings. The sea, framed as it was between the stone walls, was a beautiful bright-blue. Stepping back, I took out my phone, and snapped a picture through the archway, making sure I got a portion of the castle. Smiling, I joined Jackson for a stroll around the thirteenth-century ruins where we took photos of each other, and then numerous shots of the sea.

"You seem cheerier than you were."

"I guess you could say I let things go up here."

Jackson hugged me. "You know, I'm not fond of the statues and carvings, I saw. It's not what I expected. While good art, I still think it makes it 'touristy,' which is something, as an historian, I object to."

"When I first visited, they hadn't been created. Arthurian legend is why people come here, so I suppose it follows they want to promote that. Are you ready to go? Aunt Jane-Ann will be waiting."

"I waved to the hotel over there. I'll have to tell her."

"I took a lot of photos for her, including one of the hotel." I put my smartphone back in my crossbody bag.

"I'm starving after that climb. Where should we go?" Jackson asked as we got out of the Land Rover that had brought us to the top of the steep hill we'd hiked down earlier.

"Well, my aunt's going to want to see Tintagel. I had planned to take us to The Riverside in Boscastle, but if you're really hungry..."

"A light snack here and then on to Boscastle. You know, I really hate to say this...but I will, it's been pleasant spending the day with you without Jane-Ann's grousing the past three hours.

We retrieved my aunt, much to the obvious relief of Jeanie Beanie Penhaligan. At a tea room in the village, I instructed my aunt on how to eat scones in Cornwall, explaining it was the opposite way in Devon. "Just something to tell your friends when you get home," I told her.

And something simple to report to Gatsby Gregson, I thought.

Jackson was fascinated by the village's Old Post Office, and I must admit I thought it looked as if it came out of a *Harry Potter* novel with its wavy slate roof. The building had stood there since the fourteenth-century and had, until the Victorian times, been a manor house.

"I simply must have a photo of it, and then of myself standing in front of it," he said. "Jane-Ann, I'm sure you want one as well."

"Do you want to go inside?" I asked after taking photos of the two of them.

"Why? You said it had been a manor house for most of its time. I'm staying in one and I'll be staying in another in a couple of days. Why would I want to pay to see another one," my aunt retorted.

"Okay." Jackson took her arm. "Jessica is treating us to a meal in Boscastle, and there are a few places I want to go there, so I suggest we go on."

"But we just had tea a couple of hours ago. If I'd known that we were going to a restaurant, I wouldn't have eaten a scone. I can have those at Trevenston."

"We'll walk it off in Boscastle," I declared. "Besides, you can have a light meal. It's just that The Riverside is so nice."

"Have you brought Beckham to Trevenston?" my aunt suddenly asked on the drive to Boscastle.

"No."

"Good. I would hate for Mr. and Mrs. Euston to think you were bringing men to the house for…"

"Liam and Aisling bring friends here sometimes for the weekend. Mr. and Mrs. Euston are paid to be the property's managers. They aren't there to pass judgment on what goes on."

"Maybe they should be. Mrs. Euston and I had a talk yesterday. That place has seen plenty of action over the years, if the rumors are to be believed."

"And you, of course, believe them?"

"What rumors?" Jackson asked as we walked to the restaurant.

"Only that this place was a hotbed for," she lowered her voice, "contraband."

"Aunt Jane-Ann, please don't listen to rumors."

"It's possible, Jessica. Think of Jamaica Inn – the actual place, not the movie, or the book."

"Yes, I know, but let's just have a nice meal." We entered the restaurant and got a table by the window. "They have wonderful fish."

While we were having lunch, Jackson announced, "I've decided to go to Bath tomorrow and stay for two days, traveling out from there to see some other things. Mr. Euston got me reservations at a nice place near the center of town. I hope you don't mind that he used your name to get them."

"Not at all."

"I'll be back the day before we leave for Fielding House. Are you sure you don't want to come along for a night?"

"Bahth?" my aunt piped up between mouthfuls of fish. "I remember learning about that place. Roman. I'd like to go, Jessica."

"Lots of walking Jane-Ann, and I believe the place I'm staying has a couple of flights of stairs."

"But I would like to see the Roman ruins they have?"

I put my foot down. "No. I've been several times. One of my school friends lives near there. I think you really need to rest, and not make another trip anywhere that requires extensive walking. We'll go to Port Tristan. Please, Aunt Jane-Ann, you don't want to wear yourself out before we get to Fielding House. The children are looking forward to seeing you, and you will want to play with William Charles. We can't have you get too tired before that! I'll work on my next *Harriet Donovan*. Perhaps Mrs. Euston can share more information with you about the house and the town. No rumors, please. That should make an interesting story for the *Hilly Dale Gazette*."

Chapter Nine

Joy came the morning we finally left Trevenston Manor and began the drive to Hearthestone Vale. Although I was relieved to find acceptance of what happened to Will in Cornwall, I was also glad to leave. Jackson spent the first hour of the drive regaling us with tales of his trip to Bath.

"I'd been years ago, of course, but there's nothing like viewing this lovely city, and seeing the Roman baths again was marvelous. Of course, they cater to tourists and there's some kitsch, but overall, what a treat! What did you ladies do while I was gone? You were both in bed when I returned last night. And let me tell you that driving on these rural highways and roads after dark was no fun. So what did you do?"

"Not a damn thing," Aunt Jane-Ann exclaimed, shocking me with her expletive. I'd never heard her utter even a mild swear word.

"We went to Port Tristan for lunch and shopping, and..." I began.

"It was a disappointment," my aunt pronounced from the back seat. "Nothing to do but wander around and look in shop windows and see sailboats dotted along the harbor."

"I took a quick side-trip just to see Port Tristan on my way to Bath and I found it charming. Lovely harbor with sailboats and fishing vessels, and quaint houses and shops."

"The streets were so narrow, and we had to park in a pay lot. A pay lot in a place of that size! Mrs. Euston makes a better meal than what I had one day. I had to have fish and chips the next time we went to town."

"What did you have that you didn't enjoy?" Jackson inquired, turning around to look at her over the front seat. "I've loved all my meals."

"Some sort of meat pie."

"She means a Cornish pasty," I said.

"Whatever it was, it was *dreadful*. Some sort of turnips, onions, and ground meat."

"Swedes," I pointed out. "They were swedes."

"They weren't speaking Swedish in that restaurant. They were English-speaking but they had a strong accent."

"No, the vegetable in the pasty – that's pronounced with a short 'a,' by the way - is called a swede. It's a root vegetable, like a rutabaga."

"Then call it that. I don't like rutabagas or turnips. Please tell me you don't serve that peasant food at Fielding House."

"I'll tell Cecilia to let Mrs. Sturge know that you don't care for swedes, although I don't recall her ever making a Cornish pasty. The pasty is more of a traditional food in Cornwall, but you'll find it all over Britain." *Why on God's green earth did I share that!*

"I didn't like it, so you don't need to give me the history of a pasty or whatever you called it."

"They ate them during the *Poldark* era. Popular with miners and farmers back then," I said, just out of plain bitchiness. My only excuse was that I'd spent two whole days essentially alone with my aunt. There was no 'Jackson buffer.'

"Well, perhaps I should give them another try then," she said, thoughtfully. "I *could* serve them during a *Poldark* watching party, but without swedes, turnips, or rutabagas. I could use potatoes."

Ah, the power of suggestion. "Why, yes, you certainly could, Aunt Jane-Ann."

"Now, I know the plans at Fielding House, but what about after we leave?" Jackson inquired, thankfully stopping the Great Pasty Debate.

"I thought we'd play that by ear. There's lots to see on the way back to London. You don't have to do that, though. You can take the train from Hearthestone Vale and have a couple of days to yourself there or visit places along the way. Beck's going back on Sunday. You could take the train with him.

"Beckham is joining us at Fielding House! Jessica, that's your late husband's home. That's very inconsiderate to your family, and where does he sleep? With you?"

If I could have turned around, my aunt would have seen the scowl on my face. She'd harped about Beck and me not getting married quite a lot while I'd been with her the past few days. Every time I answered my phone or sent a text, she would ask if it was Beck. Most of the time it was one of my children, and I handed her the phone so she could speak with them.

I shouldn't have responded, but I did. "I *told* you at the Belgravia house that all guests have their own rooms when staying at Fielding-Smythe properties."

"If the floors and doors upstairs don't squeak like they do at Trevenston Manor, he could sneak to your room."

"Well, if you're so concerned, Jane-Ann, why don't you just share a room with Jessica. That would end your curiosity about her sex life, which is NO ONE's business."

"Someone has to teach people right from wrong."

"For God's sake. She's nearly fifty!"

"Jackson, changing the subject, what would you like to see if you return to London early?" I asked.

"I'd enjoy visiting Hampton Court and Westminster Abbey again. Our flight will leave from Heathrow, correct?"

"Yes, you'll be traveling first class on…"

"*Commercial* on the way home? I wasn't aware of *that*," Aunt Jane-Ann said, full of indignation.

If I hadn't been so annoyed at her interest in Beck and me and now flabbergasted by her reaction, I would have laughed. Here was a woman who had never flown in her life, nor had she lived a life of luxury, complaining that her paid holiday now included a commercial flight home in first class instead of a private jet.

"Good Heavens, Jane-Ann. Settle down. First class is an excellent way to fly. You'll enjoy it, and you might see a celebrity you recognize from Masterpiece Theater. Just sit back and enjoy the beautiful scenery as I tell you the history of the areas in which we are traveling. Now, as we enter…"

***

I unbuckled my seat belt, leaned between the front seats and tapped my aunt on her leg. "Wake up. We're stopping for a moment."

"Are we there yet?" she asked, yawning.

"Almost. We're at a service station. I'm relieving Jackson of his driving duties. Do you need to get out and…stretch?" My aunt, now accustomed to the motorway service stations, no longer wished to stop at every one of them to 'look around.' She'd found that some were simply petrol stations with food service like in America. She'd also given up her quest for a 'No Dog Fouling' sign, and had been napping since the last stop, so we were making better time than we did to Cornwall.

"Of course I do. We haven't stopped in quite a while. Just how remote is this town of yours?" she asked, opening the car door.

"Maybe fifteen miles to the house."

"Come on, Jane-Ann, I'll go with you. Jessica needs to put gasoline in the car. Do you want anything to eat?"

Jessica needs a rest, I thought while preparing to pump the petrol.

Looking around at the basic service station, she answered, "I don't think so. I assume we'll have something when we arrive at Jessica's home."

Her assumption reminded me to text Cecilia as soon as we all got in the car and give her an estimated time of arrival so that she would be there to welcome us and schedule tea.

"How are you holding up, Jessica?" Jackson asked while we waited for my aunt to exit the restroom. "Jane-Ann can be a handful."

"Tired, so I'm concerned she may be overdoing it. I want her to feel well in time for her birthday party at Fielding House Saturday night. I thought it would be fun for you, as well. The family is attending, and I've invited Elsie and a few friends."

"Are you *really* sure you want to have this party? This is Jane-Ann Simmons we're talking about. She's persnickety sometimes, and she certainly nitpicks everything."

"That's true, but I want to do something special for her. I want her to experience my life here in the hope that she will understand why I chose this country. I was prepared for all of this, but it is getting to me a little, and I can't say I'm overjoyed that the *Hilly Dale Gazette* is probably paying her for details and photographs of my life. Now that everyone already knows I'm a writer and a duchess, there's not much more to tell. I just didn't want her photographing Her Majesty and celebrities at the flower show or getting too much special treatment because of who I am."

"Any royalty or celebrities attending the party?"

"No. This isn't something they would attend anyway. They don't know her, and the party isn't a charity event."

***

Is Hearthestone Vale like this?" my aunt asked as we drove through Milkymere, a tiny village of a few rock houses and an ancient church surrounding a village green a couple of miles south of the turn-off to Fielding House.

"No, it is part of the dukedom of Hearthe, though. Hearthestone Vale is a market town. Some of the buildings date back to the fifteenth century. It's north of us, so we won't be going through there on the way to Fielding House, but I'll take you into town while we're here."

"Market town?"

"Yes, in the Middle Ages, it was a designated place that could hold markets, so as not to be confused as a village or city," I jumped in before Jackson could. "Hearthestone Vale still has 'Market Day' when stalls are set up."

"Like Hilly Dale's Farmers' Market?"

"Sort of, except that it's held in a fifteenth-century building that was once a merchant's house. The hall is all that's left, and those not in the hall set up tents outside."

"We have an indoor Farmers' Market in the old furniture store downtown. You know that, Jackson. And I know it was you who gave the money, but I haven't said a word…not one word to anyone. Gatsby Gregson must have figured it out though. EVERYONE knows it was you."

"All that matters to me is that the money I gave is going to enrich the downtown and help those property owners." I replied as I pulled up to the towers and drove slowly under the portcullis that was kept open during the day now for tourists.

Aunt Jane-Ann turned to me with an odd look and said, "Well, now I know why you had such a fascination with gates and security in Hilly Dale. What do you have behind this scary thing? A castle?"

"No, but this gatehouse was part of a thirteenth-century castle at one time. You've seen the pictures of Fielding house. It's Elizabethan."

"The Elizabethan era was..." Jackson began.

"I'm not a complete idiot, Dr. Barker," my aunt said testily. "I may not have a PhD in history, but I know about the era and I know the queen was the first Elizabeth. I watched Cate Blanchett in *Elizabeth* AND I watched *The Tudors* so I know about her father - Elizabeth's, not Cate's. I wanted to be prepared for Fielding House. And yes, I know the house is not Tudor, but Elizabeth was a Tudor."

Her declaration of knowledge stopped another history lesson, but the fact she watched *The Tudors* stunned me. While an entertaining television series, it was quite graphic at times. Aunt Jane-Ann was turning out to be a woman of many layers, and some I didn't want to remove.

"You do know that program took creative license" Jackson just had to say. "I found some things inaccurate, but they were used to create a more interesting storyline for the *viewers*. It was a good series, though."

My aunt proclaimed it 'eye-opening.' "*Shocking* at times, so it doesn't surprise me that people were poisoned at your dining room table, and worse."

"What? Who told you that?" I was hoping to keep the sordid, gruesome details of Fielding House and the old castle from my aunt.

"I did," Jackson confessed. "It adds so much to the character of the house and the property."

"At least I don't know the people involved. Not like that lewd tale your *friend* Heather James shared all the time about her husband and his mistress on the family dining table," my aunt's voice bellowed in the close confines of the car.

Oh, please, don't say it.

Thankfully, she did not. After Heather flipped-out, someone brought that incident to the attention of the *Hilly Dale Gazette*, which mortified Heather's ex-husband and the other participant in the Dining Table Debacle who happened to be his current wife, Shauna.

"And you still use your dining table. I don't know why Steve Taylor didn't fight for *his,*" Aunt Jane-Ann declared. "What a waste of a lovely piece of furniture. His parents were so angry with him, and not for having an affair – they didn't like Heather. That table had been in there family for over one hundred years."

"I've been dreaming about returning to this house and going through the library again." Jackson said.

"The hedges along this drive need trimming. Don't you have gardeners, Jessica? If you do, they are not doing a good job. Now Mr. Lucas at home would do a marvelous job here."

"We're almost to Fielding House," I said, ignoring her criticism as I drove across the rock bridge and started up the rise. As soon as we topped a hill, the E-shaped, reddish-brown stone house with its many mullioned-paned windows appeared. Off to one side, a glimpse of the lake beyond the house shimmered, and in the distance were the hills, but there was now an addition - a small white ticket booth to one side of the house with a short queue of visitors.

My aunt was quiet as we descended the hill, and then she spoiled the moment by querying, "Jessica, you have people *traipsing* through your home? Will I have no privacy here? How can you allow that? Do you approve of this?"

I didn't, and neither did my mother-in-law, but we had no say in the matter. The house, property, and all the belongings were now Alistair's and would eventually pass to my grandson William Charles, unless the antiquated primogeniture was overruled before that, and I sincerely hoped it would be. Tradition died hard, however.

I explained to my passengers that Alistair had opened the south wing with its intact part of the old castle to the public from April-October, with one week in December set for Christmas tours.

"I'll just have a word with him about *that*. A member of the family letting strangers in to see what you have? Disgraceful! Are you that desperate for money that you must do this?"

"Very old houses can become money pits. Fielding House is no exception, but I don't like the idea of opening to the public as often as

Alistair does. It requires a lot more in security and repair, which, in turn, means more money spent, so I don't quite understand the reasoning."

"Have there been issues with security?" Jackson asked.

"Yes. Some people have little respect for things and have been known to climb over the ropes and sit on the furniture. A tour guide noticed a closed door that should have been open. While her tour stood there, she opened the door and discovered a young couple having sex in the sixteenth-century bed that had once slept a member of royalty. The police were called and the couple escorted out."

"Appalling. Were they *married*?" my aunt asked.

"How would I know? And what difference does it make? They were showing total disregard for another's property. To make matters worse, they didn't even care. They did it because 'they were in the mood' and wanted to do a little role-playing as 'Duke and Duchess.' The police discovered the couple had been taking selfies while lying naked in the bed and posting them online."

"What happened?" Jackson asked.

"They were fined and had to make restitution which not only included the cleaning costs, but also for an antiques expert to come and make sure they hadn't damaged the bed. It's a priceless antique and has historical significance."

"Do you have a gift shop?"

"What?" I asked my aunt.

"A small one. You might find something for your friends."

"Are they your family things?"

"No. They're souvenirs. Items with pictures of the house, gatehouse, the church on the lake, the Keep, and so forth."

"Well, how tacky! I certainly do not want something from that gift shop for my friends. How embarrassing for them to think you are having to sell souvenirs to keep up the house."

I thought so. Pulling up next to the short wing that extended and made the center part of the 'E', I parked the car and we walked to the main entrance. I usually avoided that because of the tourists. I did it today so Aunt Jane-Ann could enter into the Great Hall from the front of the house. As we approached I heard people calling out. "Are you *somebody*? Are you the *old* duchesses?"

Jackson stifled a laugh.

"Just keep walking and don't look at them," I said.

When we entered the Great Hall, there were a few people and a tour guide wandering around, snapping pictures of the room. The guide approached me and apologized.

"I will move them on, Your Grace," she said quietly.

"Thank you." I waited until she'd hustled the group to the back and through the door. Hopefully, they wouldn't linger and would go straight through the door that led to the south wing. After I was sure no one was listening, I turned to my aunt and asked, "What do you think?"

There was no reply. For once, she was silent. I watched her look around the room in wonder, taking in the black-and-white marble-tiled floor, the dark square paneling, and then saw her looking up at the elaborately carved ceiling beams fifteen feet above us, seeing the eighteenth-century chandelier. As she had done at the townhouse, she ran her hand along a piece of furniture – this time it was the trestle table beneath the chandelier. Looking at her fingers, she nodded approvingly. Her eyes widened at the portraits of Queen Elizabeth I, Anne Boleyn, and Henry VIII hanging in a row along one wall.

"Aunt Jane-Ann?"

She turned to me and said, "I'm in awe. I knew you were a duchess, but I never expected anything like this. The house in London was elegant. Trevenston was a creaky, old manor, but this is like stepping back in time. Did Elizabeth I stay here?"

"I don't believe so. A number of houses of that era have portraits of her."

"You are immersed in history, Jane-Ann" Jackson said, just as he'd told me the first time he'd visited Fielding House for Alistair and Cecilia's wedding.

"Jackson's right. We are. These things have been here for centuries, and most in the same places. You may notice that although it's still cool up here, we don't light a fire unless we plan to use this room," I told her, nodding toward the large stone fireplace. There's concern about having a fire and tourists, unfortunately.

"What's that up there?" she asked, pointing to the minstrels' gallery located high up on the back wall.

"That was where the musicians played for the guests below. For the December evening tours, we have a quartet playing up there, and we do have a fire going. It's beautiful."

"Oh, it is," Jackson said. "I've seen this room at Christmas."

"Oh, Your Grace," the butler, Mr. Bailing cried, rushing forward. "I apologize that no one was here to greet you. Her Grace did not tell me the time you were arriving. One of the guides did not show today and His Grace asked me to step up. I'd just finished escorting a tour to the exit when I heard voices in here. Please, allow me to alert the guides that you are in the Great Hall and don't wish for tours in this room until you have left. The visitors can enter the south wing through a side door and see the Hall last.

I watched him send a text. Apparently, Cecilia hadn't passed on the information I'd sent her in mine earlier. "Isn't my daughter-in-law at home?" I asked. When I lived here, I would offer to conduct the tours in the absence of a guide on those few days we were open back then. I never would have expected a member of our staff to leave his or her duties to do something like *that* all day.

"Yes, Your Grace, she is at home."

"Very well. May I present my aunt, Mrs. Simmons, and you remember Dr. Barker. Don't bother announcing us, Mr. Bailing. She is in her sitting room, I take it?"

"Most likely, Your Grace."

"Thank you. We'll speak with her later. I trust the luggage will be brought in and placed in our rooms?"

"Yes, yours will be in the Duchess's Bedchamber, and Dr. Barker, you'll be next door. Mrs. Simmons will be on the ground floor as you requested"

"This floor, Aunt." I clarified.

"Where people traipse through? I won't have privacy."

"You will. Your room is located in the north wing – the family wing. The doors to that wing are kept locked at all times. I thought you might prefer a room on the ground floor. Less stairs. Like at Trevenston, there is no elevator."

"I climb stairs at my house every day and I climbed them in Cornwall."

"I know, but these are taller and I thought you might like to stay in The Princess's Bedchamber."

Mr. Bailing looked at me in surprise, and no wonder. We had no Princess's Bedchamber, but I did not want my aunt climbing any more stairs, especially these.

"Of course, Your Grace. The Princess's Bedchamber is where Mrs. Simmons luggage will be," he replied, not missing a beat.

After he left us, my aunt turned and said, "He didn't call you 'Your Grace' one of those times. Shouldn't you reprimand him?"

"No. It's fine. Mr. Bailing is awfully formal at times. I'd prefer he didn't use that at all, and I'm not sure Cecilia appreciates him referring to me that way either. In her presence, he calls me 'Duchess,' instead. It is *less* confusing that way. It's especially problematic when my mother-in-law is visiting though."

Jackson, my aunt, and I exited the Great Hall through the right door under the minstrel's gallery leading us to the center of the short, middle wing where I showed my aunt the large staircase that split into two at the landing leading to the upper floors of the north and south wing. From there, we turned to the right and I unlocked the door to the family wing and walked down the hallway. Opening the oak-paneled door on the left at the end of the hall, I ushered my aunt and Jackson into the newly-christened Princess's Bedchamber.

It was a small room, considering the size of others in the house, but the dark-blue velvet draperies were open over the three mullion-paned windows – one facing the back garden, one facing the north side's garden, and the other looking out on a section of the courtyard – providing more light than expected. A seventeenth-century tester bed, it's soft-blue curtains drawn back to showcase a cream-colored brocade duvet, stood next to the north-facing window. A floral wing chair with a small ottoman sat opposite in front of the fireplace. My aunt wandered around the room, again running her hands over the furniture and checking for dust.

"My mother-in-law stays here sometimes, but she resides at Raven's Roost on the estate grounds."

"Sounds like some sort of nasty bird sanctuary," Aunt Jane-Ann retorted.

"I think it sounds *delightfully* Gothic," Jackson exclaimed. "I'd love to see it."

"Which one stayed here?" my aunt asked, looking around.

"Which one?"

"The princess, Jessica." She looked at me in surprise. "What's the matter with you? Don't you even know about your own home? You certainly lived here long enough."

Oh dear. "I don't know for certain. Jackson, do you? You did a good deal of research on the family when you were here for Alistair's wedding."

"The *second* wedding I wasn't invited to," I was reminded for the umpteenth time.

"No, I don't," Jackson replied, clearly understanding that this was a made-up name for the room. "I'm sure it was someone well-known. There are portraits of royalty hanging in the house," he replied, playing along. "I suspect it was someone after Elizabeth I, though."

I gave my friend a look of sheer gratitude, before saying, "Yes, I'm sure that must be it."

"Well, it's certainly wasn't that old woman with the big nose and dressed in black with that white collar in the portrait over the fireplace," she sniped. "She's not a princess, and you would think this room would have a portrait of who stayed here. I'm glad I'll be able to close the bed curtains and shut out the view of that disapproving face. Now, the landscape over the writing desk is lovely."

While I agreed the 'old woman' was not exactly what you would expect to find, I didn't want to dig a deeper hole by exacerbating my fib, so I asked if there was anything else she needed before I showed Jackson his room.

"Is there a bathroom nearby or do I have to share like I did in Cornwall?" she asked, her face pinched in disdain, not unlike that of the woman in the portrait.

"Believe me, Jane-Ann, I'd have preferred my own as well. I'll be on another floor this time."

"The lavatory is a couple of doors away. It's the only one on this floor, and it's very small, but there is a shower, toilet, and sink. Fielding House has been modernized as much as possible without affecting its character, structure, and historical significance as a listed building. Your clothes go in the wardrobe over there."

"No closet. That's not modernized."

"At the time of various mid twentieth-century renovations, extra lavatories were deemed more important than closets and cupboards. I'll leave you to get situated. We are fortunate to have central heat and air in the family wing that was put in place thirty years ago, although we rarely use the air con. Come with me, Jackson."

"Jessica, before you go, why weren't Alistair and Cecilia here to greet us?"

"Alistair was probably working. Cecilia was in her sitting room, most likely going over menus with Mrs. Sturge the cook in preparation for our visit." Cecilia meeting with Mrs. Sturge was another fib if there ever was one. She was probably flipping through magazines or watching some reality program. She hadn't even replied to my text, and her phone was always with her.

"I can understand Alistair and his work, but for the lady of the manor not to welcome us to her home, well, I find it quite disrespectful."

For one of the few times in my life, I agreed with her. It *was* disrespectful. My daughter-in-law either hadn't understood or hadn't taken to her duties, one of which was overseeing the household, if only in a cursory manner. Mrs. Sturge still relied on me when I was in residence and had even been known to contact me at Lilac House if there was an issue or a need for confirmation. She wasn't the only member of staff to do that. Mrs. Thomas the house manager also did. The latter I texted to request tea in the courtyard before escorting Jackson upstairs.

Chapter Ten

Looking fresh and pretty in her sunny-yellow ankle pants and white cotton sweater, her hair and makeup perfect, Cecilia sat at the black wrought-iron table watching my aunt, and me walk across the courtyard to join her. Only when we were within a couple of feet did she rise from the chair to greet us.

"Carola," she said, kissing me on the cheek before turning to my aunt, "Mrs. Simmons, how lovely you are able to join us this week."

"Do I curtsy?" my aunt whispered. I shook my head. *Definitely not!*

"Where is Dr. Barker?" Cecilia inquired, flipping her shiny blonde hair behind an ear. I noticed her shade had lightened considerably since I saw her a month ago.

"He wanted to unpack and clean up after the drive." I was pretty sure he wanted an hour of peace and quiet. I wished I could retreat for a while, but that wasn't going to happen.

Cecilia smiled and sat down, indicating we should do the same. "I'm surprised he didn't choose to stay in London. He has visited Fielding House before. I prefer London. So much to do. It can be a bore here." She looked at my aunt. "We're used to tourists traipsing about, so if you wish to view the house, Mrs. Simmons, you're welcome to do so. I'm sure one of the staff will show you...or perhaps Carola will do the honors. I would, but I still get lost."

"That's kind of you...Duchess," my aunt replied awkwardly, looking at me for confirmation.

I had told her not to use 'Your Grace.' Aunt Jane-Ann was family. 'Duchess' first was fine and we could go from there, but my daughter-in-law did not suggest my aunt call her 'Cecilia,' as a gracious member of the family would have done. I might need a quiet word with her.

Two young woman I didn't recognize served us tea, small sandwiches, and petit-fours on a three-tiered sterling silver stand. Cecilia poured from the blue, gold, and white teapot into matching cups.

"Lovely service," complimented my aunt.

"Yes, it is. Quite famous maker. Lomonosov. Imperial Russian porcelain. 22 karat gold in the design. It is based on Catherine the Great's dinnerware. We, of course, have an entire set," she over-informed. "Now, Mrs. Simmons, like Carola, I presume you don't take milk in your tea. The *American* way, isn't it. Plenty of sugar for you? Isn't that the way you Americans take it?"

"Like my niece, I like my tea without either. I prefer coffee, however." I recognized an edge to her voice. My aunt was a stickler for manners - other people's manners, that is - and Cecilia had neglected to use her own.

"Oh, like Mr. Hailey," Cecilia said, pouring a drop of milk into her tea. I was surprised she wasn't having one of the two women standing nearby pour, if only for effect.

"Oh, does Mr. Hailey spend a lot of time here?" Aunt Jane-Ann inquired, her teacup nearly to her lips.

Before Cecilia could respond, I asked, "Will Jackson have something sent to him in his room? We've had a long drive."

"Certainly. Do that, Magdalena," she ordered one of the women. "How remiss of me not to check on his needs and arrange something for *him*. We shall help ourselves here. See to Dr. Barker. You're both excused." Cecilia dismissed them with a wave of her hand.

"*I* alerted Mrs. Thomas about tea, so all Magdalena will need to do is take a tray to his room. Have you hired more staff, Cecilia?" I asked, preparing a plate for my aunt.

"Oh, yes. I told Alistair we simply *must* have more help, what with the tourists making everything so dirty, and we do need more security to guard the items in the rooms."

"I heard about the couple having sex in the antique bed," Aunt Jane-Ann divulged, in a not-too-quiet voice.

"Carola! You shared that with her? "

"Yes, she did. It was on the way here when Jessica told Jackson and me all about the tourists visiting. I found it shocking."

"It was disgusting," Cecilia stated a little too vehemently. "They were chavvy."

"I should say it was," Aunt Jane-Ann agreed. "Chavvy?"

"Trashy wannabes is what I suppose you might say," Cecilia informed her in a bored manner, as if my aunt should be familiar with common British slang.

"Cecilia!" I exclaimed.

"It's true. That is what those two were."

"Aunt Jane-Ann, the slang word is a pejorative. Please don't use it."

Cecilia gave me a quizzical look. "Your aunt referred to you as 'Jessica.' Why?"

"You know that is my first name and what I was called until I married Will. Aunt Jane-Ann has known me by that name since I was born. It stands in *family* situations." I hoped she would take the hint and suggest that my aunt refer to her by her name, but she did not.

"Oh, well…"

"I'm sure it was shocking to learn of that couple desecrating a centuries-old bed, but that's what happens when you let strangers into your home," interrupted Aunt Jane-Ann.

I reached over and touched my aunt's leg.

"Jessica, what are you touching me for? I'm only stating what you told me. You said you didn't think it necessary to have the house open as much as it is now."

Thank goodness my phone pinged. "It's Aisling finally getting back in touch," I told them. "Please excuse me for a moment."

Hi Mum. See you this Friday, she texted.
Looking forward to it.
Does Aunt know?
Not yet.
James is coming.
That's fine.
Liam at home?
No. Jordan will be here.
Liam better watch out. James is bringing his brother.
Which one?
Jago the heir. Aka Shagger.
Keep that to yourself. Had to explain 'chavvy' to A.J.A. just now.
LOL! Better text Liam.

You text him. He listens to you. Try to be on time for the do.

"I apologize. I normally don't like to take calls or messages when I'm with others, but Aisling has been busy at school, and I don't hear from her as much."

"Is she still with the Earl of Cradleburn's *youngest* son?" Cecilia looked pained at the thought. "She could do so much better."

"She and James Walkstone are quite happy together. You would like him, Aunt. He's from a good family. He'll be accompanying her this weekend."

"Really, Carola? Now you're inviting your daughter's friends."

I stood up. "Cecilia, may I speak with you for a moment, please? We'll be right back, Aunt."

When we were out of earshot just inside the room leading to the courtyard, I snapped, "I'd appreciate it if you were more gracious in front of my aunt. Need I remind you that Alistair considers her his family. And, if my daughter wishes to bring her boyfriend or any of her friends to her home, that is her prerogative, as long as she clears it with Alistair. Who she dates is also her business. She has no *need* to climb a social ladder. She is a duke's daughter."

Cecilia flushed, knowing that I considered her mother a social climber. "I am The Duke's wife and I am in charge here, so…"

"You are not in charge here. Alistair is. Unless you have a job, or your own private income, you are dependent on *him*. Aisling is his sister; Jane-Ann Simmons is his aunt."

"Well, she's not really. Mummy says if you're not a blood relation…"

"I have news for you," I said quietly, "*You're* not a blood relation, and your mother *certainly* isn't. You would both do well to remember that. Being a duchess means you married *into* the family and are held to high standards; it does not mean that you are allowed to act like an utter cow in front of guests. You did not even come out of your sitting room to greet us, nor did you arrange for tea."

"I didn't know you had arrived."

"I texted you the time we'd arrive. Mr. Bailing wasn't even there. He had to give a tour! You should have been doing that. If you don't do anything else here, at least fill-in and help out. Now, I suggest we rejoin my aunt and you treat her with respect and courtesy."

Back at the table, I explained that I was telling Cecilia about Jackson's dietary issues. It was obvious by her expression, that she did not believe a word of that. She eaten with Jackson a number of times. To her credit, she held her tongue. Suitably chastised, Cecilia tried to play hostess by offering my aunt a refill on her tea. The tea was cold, so she sent a message to bring more. I was surprised she didn't have a bell handy.

"Cecilia, I've brought gifts for William Charles," I said in an overly-cheerful tone. "How is he? I haven't had any updates or photos for a week."

"He is perfect, Carola," she replied stiffly. "Miss Hawkins dotes on him. I hardly get a minute with him without her presence. She takes her job *so* seriously."

"A nanny, of course," my aunt said.

"*Everyone* in our set has one. It's just so trying to find the right one, but we did get a gem from a nanny school. It's not the one where the Cambridges got theirs, but it still has quite a good reputation. Miss Hawkins is brilliant. Never married and has dedicated her life to helping those of us who want to do all we can for our children but find ourselves too busy with our work and other endeavors."

Brother! "Miss Hawkins is excellent, Aunt. I know you'll like her."

"I'm looking forward to meeting William Charles. I've brought him a few things from Arkansas."

"Isn't that thoughtful." Cecilia smiled sweetly and took a sip of her tea, now hot, thanks to Magdalena who had hurried out with a silver teapot and refilled the one on the table. "Stay nearby," Cecilia commanded. "We'll need refills." Apparently, she had lost interest in playing hostess.

Chapter Eleven

"Aunt Jane-Ann!" Alistair cried, hurrying across the family living room and hugging her. "Jackson! So happy to see you. Sorry I wasn't here to welcome you. I was on the estate with the groundskeeper and security guard. Someone tried to break into the Keep again and managed to get some sort of metal pick stuck in the lock."

"You would allow them out there alone," I reminded him. "We talked about this when you chose to open the grounds as well as the house."

"Mum, you know if we deny them the old Keep *and* the church, we will be just another house."

"I think you ought to have a guard at both of those places, or at the very least give guided tours. The church is precious to all of us, and I don't want to see the gravestones being *assisted* on their way to rubble. You can't expect Thor to do the patrols any longer with tourists about. He's getting old and people being what they are, you just never know what they might do to him."

Thor was our Landseer, a dog that was, in some circles, considered to be a type of Newfoundland. Black-and-white Thor weighed in at one-hundred-seventy-two pounds. He was friendly, unless he considered you a trespasser which is what he'd sense the tourists were.

"Mr. Bailing is interviewing potential guides, and I've hired an extra guard for the church. Thor is well-protected now. His house is fenced."

"Yes, he's stuck in a pen," I said.

"Not all the time, Mum. He gets his run and I do not allow him out there in bad weather."

Cecilia shrugged. "Thor is old, and I don't appreciate that you bring him in the house, Alistair. He scares me sometimes, and he could easily break things, or hurt our child." She had never taken to Thor, nor the dog to her.

"He's my dog, Cecilia. If I thought he happened to be a danger to you or William Charles he would remain outside, but I refuse to keep him in that pen all the time. He was here first…I mean, before the tourists."

And before you, Cecilia, I thought. Thor was never left alone with William Charles either, although there had been no hint of aggression.

Aunt Jane-Ann gave Alistair a thorough once-over from the top of his dark hair, to his hazel eyes, to his jeans, to his work boots. "Just where is this Keep? In a jungle? You look attired for that."

Alistair laughed. "No, Aunt, but it is in a wooded area. I'll take you out there while you're here. It's something to see. Thirteenth-century and the last bastion for those who lived in the castle that was here. You can also see some of the castle in the house's south wing. One of us will take you."

"Liam, probably, if he's able to be here. He loves to take guests to both places and tell them all sorts of ghost stories. Don't believe a word he says, Aunt."

"After seeing inside the Keep, *I* believe those stories," Jackson shivered. "I even researched some of the things that happened there, and they are TRUE."

"I hope Liam will have everything arranged and can join us," Alistair said. "He's working hard."

"Aisling texted that you better have him here day after tomorrow."

"Oh," Alistair glanced at his aunt. "Yes, I'd better get on that later."

"He texts every now and then. I don't know why you sent him up there for such a long stay, Alistair." I was upset about that. I wanted my aunt to see him."

"He's only been gone ten days – at least I think that's about right. It has been taking longer than I'd like though. He's purchased the livestock, but he's in the Highlands now and is going to some remote places. I'd hoped to find a location with a country house or lodge for business purposes, but the weather has not been cooperating, so…"

"Where is my little nephew? I want to see him," Aunt Jane-Ann interrupted.

"I'd love to meet him. I've only seen photos," Jackson said.

Alistair looked at his wife. "Ceci? Do you think Miss Hawkins will allow us to have William Charles for a bit?"

85

"I'll go get him," I offered, standing up. "I've brought presents for him. They're in the blue tote over there. Aunt Jane-Ann has some things for him, too."

"Oh, why don't we all go up to the nursery then. He can open them up there and won't make a mess down here," Cecilia suggested, looking around the extremely tidy room.

Kneeling down beside her chair, I murmured, "I think you can make an *exception* for my aunt, as you do for Alistair's grandmother, and your own. My aunt's nearly eighty-two and uses a cane sometimes. The stairs to the nursery are too many for her to climb."

"Yes, of course. I'll text Miss Hawkins."

The pleasant-looking, middle-aged Miss Hawkins had a firm hold on William Charles's hand when they entered the room. My grandson was chomping at the bit to get loose. I'd just seen him in person a month prior but he was growing up so fast. I was sure he was taller and that his dark-brown hair was thicker. Those twinkling blue eyes gave him a mischievous look that was very appealing, if I say so myself. When he saw me, he pulled free of Miss Hawkins and ran as only a toddler can over to me first thing.

"Can-Can," he cried holding out his arms for me to pick him up, which, of course, I did. 'Can-Can' was his name for me. We thought it came from him hearing the names Carola and Granny, the latter was how Damaris referred to me in his and everyone else's presence. I was thankful he chose 'Can-Can.'

"How is my sweet boy?" I gave him a kiss on the cheek.

"Good."

"I have some presents for you."

"Prezzis?"

"Yes, they are over by Mummy." I set him on the floor and he walked quickly over to Cecilia who was sitting in a comfortably-padded modern chair near the fireplace. Cecilia didn't bat at any eye that there was a small decorative fire burning as her son hurried up to her and began pulling paper out of the tote bag to find the few items I'd brought, but Miss Hawkins noticed and quickly crossed the floor, standing near enough to grab him if necessary.

"How's my little Earl today?" Cecilia asked, reaching for him, but he squirmed out of her grasp and resumed tearing up the paper to reach the bottom of the tote where a soft toy resembling Thor awaited, along with a couple of shirts. He hugged the toy to his chest.

"Earl? I thought his name was William," my aunt said, looking puzzled.

"Oh, it is, but William Charles has my secondary title of 'Earl of Ponder.' Cecilia calls him 'Earl.' It's a kind of nickname," Alistair replied.

I noticed Cecilia only called him that in the presence of guests. Alistair called him W.C. which made me laugh and Cecilia cringe. W.C. was short for water closet, an old term for where toilets were located. While Jackson would have found that funny, I knew my aunt wouldn't,

"Ponder is a quaint village just to the north west of us. Pondermere is the lake you could see as we topped the hill on the way up the drive. When we take a trip to the Keep, I'll show you the old church where Will's memorial service was held. It's right on the lake."

"Oh, the Prince of Wales attended that. I'd like to see the place," she said. "Now, let me look at this little man. I'm your Aunt Jane-Ann and look what I have for you."

Reaching into her red tote, she pulled out a child-sized, red-and-white Arkansas Razorbacks short-sleeved tee-shirt and a small, red football with a Razorback painted on each side. My grandson walked over to her. "Do you know what animal that is, William Charles?" she asked. When he shook his head, she continued, "It's a Razorback. A wild pig."

"Pigs on farm," my grandson answered.

"That's right, but these run wild. They're dangerous."

"Mrs. Simmons, please don't scare my son," Cecilia admonished.

"She's not scaring him. Leave it alone," Alistair told her.

"But, Alistair. Wild pigs?"

"He sees pigs on the tenants' farms. He just said that."

"But not wild ones. I don't want him scared."

"He's seen wild boars. Forget it. This is a university mascot."

"Don't be ridiculous. I'm not scaring him. I'm showing him something that my state is famous for. His father is correct. It's a football team's mascot. I have something for you, too, Alistair."

"American football, Ceci. It's like a religion there. Everyone loves the Razorbacks. I went to a game once when I was in Arkansas, right Mum."

"You did. My parents took Alistair, Liam, Aisling, Will, and me to a game. It was great fun."

Rooting to the bottom of her red tote, Aunt Jane-Ann drew out a hat -a classic, red plastic one in the shape of a Razorback, complete with white tusks. "It's known as a 'hog hat' and you'll see them at football games."

Alistair immediately put it on. "How do I look? Liam has one of these, I believe, but he took it to university with him."

"Fun-nee," William Charles said pointing his finger at his father's head.

Cecilia looked green when my aunt handed her a women's white sweatshirt – a size too big - with the red razorback on the front of it. "How...unique," she managed to say. "Thank you, Mrs. Simmons."

"Hold it up," Alistair told her.

"Oh, Lord," Jackson cried, grabbing his phone and taking a picture of Alistair and a quick one of Cecilia before she dropped the sweatshirt.

"Now, let's call the hogs, shall we, William Charles," my aunt cried, just as excited as she was the day she saw Judi Dench, Her Majesty, and Their Royal Highnesses.

Right there in our family living room - a room that had entertained a variety of nobility in its over four-hundred-fifty years - my aunt began the famous cheer. On the second and third time through, William Charles had caught on, raising his arms and finally managing the entire cheer, giggling at 'Pig Sooie,' each time. Alistair sat down on the floor so his son could get a closer look at the hat he wore.

"What on earth is that hideous cry?" A voice cut through the laughter. "And Alistair, what is that on your head?"

Turning, I saw a dark-haired, overly made-up woman in expensive, tailored white trousers and a muted-green jacket over a patterned silk blouse. *Damaris Hempstead*!

"Oh, Mummy, Mrs. Simmons was teaching our little earl an American *cheer*. As you can see, she's brought... presents. You're early for your visit. I thought you were coming at the weekend."

"Presents? Oh, I see. I *thought* you could use a hand with the extra guests, Cecilia." She looked from my aunt to Jackson, to me, and then at Alistair. "Again, what *is* that thing on your head?"

"A hog hat. We're learning a cheer," Alistair intervened. "And it's fun, isn't it W.C.?" My grandson giggled and cried 'sooie' again.

"How...unique," Damaris uttered the exact words her daughter had used.

"It is, isn't it, Damaris," I interjected. "It's special to my home state."

"Interesting, I'm sure. Next time you're visiting a pig farm in Arkansas, Alistair, you'll know what to do. Come to Nana, Earl." William Charles ignored her and concentrated on the cheer he'd just learned and was holding the little football while yelling 'sooie.' Everyone laughed but Cecilia and her mother.

"As fascinating as the traditions are in your home state, Carola, are you suggesting that we bring the hillbilly antics into Fielding House? Cecilia, what did we talk about after Carola went to the States?"

"I know, Mummy, but Carola's aunt brought presents."

"Hillbilly things from Hillybilly Dale's Duchess and her aunt."

"Mummy!" For once, Cecilia seemed shocked at her mother's rudeness.

I wasn't. When it came to Damaris anything could happen, but I didn't want my aunt humiliated. My greatest fear was that Alistair was discovering his wife wasn't who he thought he'd married.

"You know I'm right, Cecilia. We discussed this. Come to Nana, William Charles."

"No Gran-nee. I want Can-Can," he cried and ran straight toward me, and wanted to be picked up again. I obliged. "How's my favorite grandson?" I asked and gave him a hug. William Charles giggled.

"Oh for Heaven's sake. You are not his grandmother. I am. You're merely Alistair's *stepmother*."

"Now see here, Damaris, you are out-of-line," Alistair remonstrated. "Mum, I apologize. We've had this discussion before, Damaris."

"It's fine, Alistair. I'd prefer not to discuss this now." I tilted my head toward William Charles who was still in my arms. "Say 'thank you,' to Auntie for your gifts."

Obeying, he said in his 'inside' voice, enunciated very well for someone two-and-a-half, "Thank you."

"You're very welcome, young man," my aunt answered. "*You* have good manners."

"But, Mum, that was..."

"Not now, Alistair," I said, using the disapproving mother look and tone of voice. It still worked, even on thirty-three-year-old dukes. I placed my grandson on the carpet and handed him the football which he proceeded to throw.

"Miss Hawkins, will you please take William Charles to the nursery?" Alistair lifted his son and carried him to the nanny. "Say goodbye to your grandmothers."

"Bye, Can-Can."

"And to your other grandmother?" Alistair coached.

"Bye, Gran-nee."

Damaris grimaced at that. Her ploy to get him to call me 'Granny' had backfired. Cries of 'Sooie' could be heard before she closed the door and turned back to the adults in the room.

"Now that the distraction is over, Cecilia, I talked to Carina Stallcott yesterday and she recommended we go to Mustique for a holiday," she said, taking a seat in the chair nearest her daughter. "I'm sure you'll easily be able to book something if you use your title, Alistair. Carina said so."

"Mustique? I don't think so, Damaris," Alistair objected. "Using my title to bump someone from their own holiday anywhere is something I don't do, and I highly doubt that would happen on Mustique anyway. There are far wealthier and far more important people than I who visit the island."

"But Alistair," Cecilia pleaded, "It would be a wonderful holiday. The Cambridges go there, and celebrities, too. Carina says it's private and peaceful. We *need* a family holiday, and William Charles would love the beach."

"That's correct. *We* need a family holiday– you, me, and our son, and no one else. A private one, but *not* in Mustique. We can find a beach or seaside anywhere. We could to Cornwall, or what about Bournemouth?"

"Alistair, be reasonable. Cornwall at that dreary house? Bournemouth? Mustique is where," Damaris paused midsentence and then said, "What is that mess on the carpet? And, please, take that hideous thing off your head."

Aunt Jane-Ann looked at Alistair and then at her discarded gifts - the tee shirt, sweatshirt, and football - scattered on the faded Persian rug. Getting up, I gathered the items and put them in my aunt's red tote, giving Damaris a cold look as I did so. "He loved them and the cheer you taught him," I murmured to my aunt. "I'm sure Cecilia liked her sweatshirt too."

Completely out-of-character, my aunt suddenly deflated and said quietly, "I don't know what I did wrong. The gifts represent my home state."

"Nothing. *You* did nothing wrong, and under the circumstances, you have been very gracious," I replied before standing up and addressing the others. "I don't think this is the time to discuss your personal matters or a holiday at all, Alistair. Jackson and your aunt are present, and they are here to see you, William Charles, and…Cecilia."

"My apologies to you both. So, Aunt, how has your first trip to England been so far?

"Beyond my expectations. I loved The Chelsea Flower Show. It was perfection. I saw Her Majesty and the Duke and Duchess of Cambridge." My aunt's eyes lit back up at the memory, "And Judi Dench and an actor from *Downton Abbey* were there - not together, of course. They were attending the same day."

"I imagine it was quite the experience for you. Oh, my friend saw you, Carola, and that Elsie Tattersdown." Damaris shared. "Cecilia should have attended, but she had other duties to perform. How lovely you could take her place, Carola."

What other duties. Shop and take holidays? I bit my tongue for Alistair's sake. "Elsie is *Lady* Toddle," I said, driving home the point that Damaris had no title.

"I'm aware of that. I asked her about being on *The Wives and Girlfriends of Nobility*, but she declined."

"Sensible woman, Lady Toddle is," a strong voice with the trace of an Irish lilt called from the doorway. "Disgraceful concept." We all turned to look.

Escorted by Mr. Bailing was a short, trim woman in her eighties and she did not look happy. My mother-in-law Josephine Fielding-Smythe, the eldest Duchess of Hearthe had arrived. She had never been fond of Damaris.

"Now, what have I missed? What is happening here?" she asked.

What was happening was that Damaris was either drunk or wanting to cause a scene, which made me wonder if she wore a hidden camera and microphone. Given her penchant for revealing family business, I would not put it past her.

"Nothing, Nan. Just a surprise to see Damaris before the weekend," Alistair said, standing up and giving his grandmother a kiss.

"Surprise? Why? She's always here, and it didn't look like 'nothing' to me. What's that on your head?"

Alistair reached up to touch the hog hat. "A present from Aunt Jane-Ann. Something special in her state."

"Interesting. Bend down and let me see it." He did and Josephine took it off his head and examined it further. "Clever. A wild pig with tusks and a spiky back, but why is it red?"

"School colors, Nan. Red and white. It's an American football team's mascot."

"Were I a member of the opposing team, *I* wouldn't want to engage in a battle with something like that. You must be Carola's aunt. I'm her mother-in-law," Josephine declared, walking straight to Aunt Jane-Ann, who stood. The two women sized each other up, favorably it seemed because my mother-in-law asked my aunt what had happened.

"*That* woman," my aunt replied, nodding in Damaris's direction, "insulted my home state, ridiculed the gifts I brought, and disparaged both my relationship and Carola's to your grandson and great-grandson."

"Is this true, Damaris? You insulted Alistair's mother and her aunt?"

"She's not his mother, and her aunt was teaching William Charles some obnoxious cheer."

"I heard it. Bailing and I stood outside the door and listened to what was going on. I do believe 'sooie' is used to call pigs in some places in the States. I can only think that might help when at some stage in his life William Charles is called upon to judge livestock." Josephine looked over the top of her glasses at Damaris. "And that reality show? Not that again. I forbid it." My mother-in-law was on a roll. "Cecilia, did you know about this?"

"Well, I…"

"Ceci, did you know? We talked about this before the marriage and again just a few months ago. You know how I feel about this preposterous notion of your mother's. It will embarrass the family."

"Alistair, I'm bored here. I need something to do. Mummy thought it would be fun. Light, entertaining."

"Mummy *thought* it would get her some publicity and attention," Josephine mimicked the whine in Cecilia's voice. "If you would find something to occupy your time, such as charity work in Hearthestone Vale or a hobby, or even giving the tours of this place – tours I object to, but it is not my decision - you might not find life here such a bore."

"She's not wrong, Cecilia," Damaris spoke up, "but *I* believe you should find something you *want* to do."

"No one cares what you believe, *Mrs.* Hempstead," an annoyed Josephine declared. "It must get a little windy riding the coattails of this family. As for my great-grandson, I know you and Cecilia call him 'Little Earl' around others. Stop it at once. It's crass. His name is William Charles. William after my late son and Charles after Carola's late father. Show some respect."

"Josephine, my daughter does a marvelous job. It's not easy to put up with a *blended* family. Carola *is* Alistair's stepmother. That is a fact, you can't change."

"My niece has been the *only* mother Alistair has known," my aunt returned fire. *She* is an accomplished woman. She's an author, for goodness' sake. She didn't sit on her behind ordering people around and taking holidays, which is what it sounds like from what I've heard in the short time I've been here. Just like me, my niece came from Arkansas, so when you insult that state, you're not just insulting me, you are insulting her, Liam, and Aisling. Arkansas is part of Liam and Aisling's heritage, just as much as the nobility is, and those two were *born* into nobility."

"Mrs. Simmons, I salute you!" my mother-in-law exclaimed. "That is exactly how I feel about this. Cecilia, you are The Duchess of Hearthe because you are married to The Duke of Hearthe. You have duties that you are expected to conduct. Carola has been doing them for you. And, *Mrs.* Hempstead, if I see anything about this family again written by one of your gossip columnist friends, I will call in a few favors and sue, and Alistair you need to gain better control over your wife. Now, I'm ready for my dinner. Dr. Barker, will you escort me, please?"

"Delighted," he replied.

"Now, how has your trip been this time?" she asked as they led the way out of the room.

"Cecilia, that's not protocol. Alistair should go first," Damaris muttered loud enough for me to hear.

"We don't stand on ceremony when it's family," Alistair retorted. "Aunt Jane-Ann?" He extended his arm and escorted her to dinner, leaving Cecilia, Damaris, and me to follow. It didn't bother me, but it certainly did the other two.

To say dinner in the formal dining room was awkward was an understatement. I wondered if those who had been poisoned at the table were as obnoxious as Damaris.

***

"Oh Beck, it was an awful scene," I told him when we spoke that night. "Alistair and Cecilia left in the middle of dinner and had a terrible row which Damaris, Josephine, Jackson, Aunt Jane-Ann, and I could hear while having our meal. The entire *staff* could hear it. Damaris tried to get up to 'help,' but Josephine emphatically told her to sit down and my aunt added 'and shut up' to it."

"And did she?"

"Oh yes. Two indignant eighty-something-year-old women telling her what to do was quite effective, and it was extremely funny. Jackson and I tried hard to keep our own faces stern."

"Are the party plans still on?"

"Yes. I sincerely hope Cecilia did not allow her mother to invite those common women with whom she associates. Ever since I moved back, I've had a nagging suspicion that Cecilia, probably encouraged by her mother, had her eyes on the prize well before she started dating Alistair. She'd been seeing his best friend for some time and then broke it off. I hope that becoming a duchess wasn't why she married. She looked so in love on her wedding day."

"Some people play a good game. You know that. Remember my ex-wife Bianca, and then there was Heather James. She fooled several people."

"Heather was mentally-ill and drinking on top of that. At least Bianca wanted you."

"Yeah, for prestige in high school, and then later when we re-connected, for money. From what you've said and what I've observed being around Cecilia, she wants the luxuries in life, but it seems that once she married, she felt she didn't need to do anything else."

"That was pointed out to her by Aunt Jane-Ann and was applauded by Josephine."

"Wow! Didn't Cecilia work at an art gallery in London before marriage?"

"Yes, and while she couldn't do that up here, she could volunteer to give tours of Fielding House or open a gallery in Hearthestone Vale. It's not a podunk village. It's located in a beauty spot. Not only do we have regular tourists, there are specific tours for artists. If I'm not mistaken, there is a local group that gets together for painting trips, and not just around here. They've traveled through Europe together. She could open a gallery for them to showcase and sell their work. And if anything, she could pay attention to her son a bit more. The child is going to think Miss Hawkins is his mother, and I'm not certain he cares for his other grandmother." I told him how William Charles had ignored Damaris and run to me, which seemed to be what set the other woman off.

"Damaris is another jealous woman, but unlike old Heather James, she has the wherewithal to do something about it. Yeah, I know Heather did something, but Damaris has some money and connections, so she wouldn't have to resort to anything physical. She's into sabotage, and with her friends writing for tabloids, she can really make that happen."

"Speaking of that, I forgot to tell you that Isabel Allensworth who wrote a couple of those Hillbilly articles approached me at The Chelsea Flower Show."

"Did you talk to her?"

"Barely, and my responses were sweetly-said."

"I'm sure they were. The party is going to be awkward, I'm afraid."

"Oh, I hope not. I want my aunt to have a nice time. She can be a pain, but she's family."

"I understand, but speaking from experience with awkward family matters, I hope Alistair was smart enough to have a prenuptial agreement with custody, along with financial settlements, if they divorce. They haven't been married long, but once Damaris and her husband get wind of anything, they'll be sure to try and get all they can for Cecilia.

"And Damaris would milk the publicity. You can rest assured, though, that with the good firm of Poleduck & Poleduck and Mr. Hartfield's accounting team, the pre-nup is there and it's covered all bases. I've got to get some sleep. I love you."

"I love you, too. See you this weekend."

Lying back on the pillows, I looked around The Duchess's Bedchamber thinking how if I hadn't been staying in here, Damaris would have been. I was willing to bet her nose was out of joint having to sleep in one of the smaller rooms on the upper floor. She was only the mother of a duchess, but I WAS a duchess, and there were times that she needed to be reminded of that. I imagine tonight was one of those, and it made me smile.

Chapter Twelve

We had a tense early breakfast with a small war of words between Aunt Jane-Ann and Damaris after my aunt 'innocently' asked *Mrs. Hempstead* if she'd slept well. An emphatic "No" confirmed that Damaris always stayed in The Duchess's Bedchamber when she visited and was unhappy being demoted.

After breakfast, I needed some fresh air. Setting off in one of the available golf carts, my aunt and I toured the grounds, eventually ending up near the graveyard. "We'll have to walk from here," I said, helping her out of the cart. "The path is rough, but it's a pleasant walk and we'll get some exercise too."

"I'm sorry about last night and this morning, but there's something about that Mrs. Hempstead I don't like, and I find Alistair's wife a social climber just like her mother. You never mentioned that about Cecilia, and she has yet to invite me to use her given name. Am I always to address her as 'Duchess?' It seems very offensive. *You* did not do that in Hilly Dale after everyone found out. Social climbing is a very unattractive trait."

In Hilly Dale, my aunt was the epitome of a social climber. She wanted desperately to fit into what passed as society in that small town, and she had managed to do so. Damaris Hempstead was a different matter, particularly if she was using her daughter's marriage to Alistair as a stepping stone.

Aunt Jane-Ann walked with her hand on my arm and used her other one to hold on to her cane while we strolled down the path to the church. Reaching out with the cane to brush a twig off a gravestone, she commented on the barely visible names and dates. "These stones are crumbling. Don't you have a service that maintains this cemetery?"

"Just our groundskeepers. Some of these stones date back centuries, so there's not a great deal of restoration that can be done. Hopefully, with the guards Alistair says he has hired to patrol the grounds, there will be no more people trying to do gravestone rubbings, particularly where there is a carving on the stones. That used to be all the rage, and it's bad enough, but to chip pieces off the stones for souvenirs is a desecration, and we have had that happen."

"How ghoulish!"

"I think so."

Gazing around the graveyard, Aunt Jane-Ann blurted, "Where's your husband buried?"

I turned her to face one of several mausoleums that could be seen among the trees to the north. "He's in there." I pointed to the farthest one.

"I'm glad, for once, to see they all have sturdy doors and padlocked gates. If they were so low as to chip a piece off a headstone, I'd hate to think what tourists would do if they got in one of those. Are there tomb effigies in any of those mausoleums?"

"Yes, the older ones. You can tell those from the outside condition. We try to keep any cracks patched."

"Well, I suppose that you'll be in there with your husband. What about Beckham? Where will he go?"

I didn't answer that. Although my aunt had stood up for me in front of Damaris, there were times she could appall me with her candor. "If you look right over there, you will see Lake Pondermere and at the end of the peninsula," I said, "is the church where Will and I had a secret wedding before the one in Hearthestone Vale. The only ones present were my parents, Will, me, and the vicar. It is also where we had Will's memorial service."

"What a beautiful setting. It reminds me of one used in some program I saw on PBS a while back. Was it here?"

"No, this house has not been used as a location."

"And yet you allow tourists to regularly tromp through for money."

I didn't allow anyone to 'regularly tromp through.' She had a point. At least a film location would bring more attention than simply opening to the public.

"That bell tower up there, does the bell ring?"

Did it? Over a year after our parting of the ways in Hilly Dale, Beck had turned up one evening while I was standing by this church. It was here I learned he'd crossed an ocean to personally speak to me and voice his feelings. At that time, I thought I heard the bell ringing even though there was no wind. The bell was heavy, requiring two people to pull on the rope to swing it. Beck said he heard it as well. To me, the ringing had signified that my late husband was giving me permission to move on, but at the time I wasn't completely sure I would move on with Beck, given our locations.

After he moved to London with his job, our relationship developed and we were happy, though I still missed Will, especially here. While I'd missed him at Trevenston Manor, that house was conducive to depressive thoughts, and I was glad to see the back of it. I'd return to Cornwall, but not there.

"Let's go inside." I suggested when we reached the church's heavy, studded front door. Unlocking it, we walked down the aisle, taking a seat on the front row to the right. "I sat here at the service."

"Where did the Prince of Wales sit?"

"Right behind me."

My aunt got up. Turning in my seat, I cried, "Wait, where are you going?"

"I want to sit where His Royal Highness sat so I can tell my friends that I, Jane-Ann Simmons, rested my behind in the exact place where a future king rested his. It's just like when Rose, the Bellamy's maid, on *Upstairs, Downstairs* plopped down in the chair where King Edward VII was to sit at dinner that night! I hope you're not going to give me a stern talk like Mr. Hudson gave Rose!"

I laughed - laughed in the church where in the past few years I'd sat and cried, and it was due to my aunt's new fascination with Masterpiece Theater and PBS. Traveling with my aunt had been puzzling. She still had that sharpness, snobbery, fight, and candor about her, but there was now a sense of fun showing occasionally. I'd seen it with my grandson, and at The Chelsea Flower Show we'd attended, and now here, at this church. Perhaps she was happier in a nice home, and being able to afford some extras, or maybe it was just because she was in a different country and wasn't in control of everything. Either way, I felt my spirits lighten around her, just a little.

After a few minutes sitting, we got up and my aunt took a photo of the spot on the pew she had shared with the Prince of Wales, and then asked me to take a photo of her sitting in the spot. She also made photos of the church which seemed more along the lines of normal.

"My friends will be so envious," she exclaimed when we stepped outside. Sitting on the little bench I'd had placed in memory of Will, I pointed out the general northwest direction across the lake where Hearthestone Vale was located and explained that beyond the hills to the west was the Irish Sea. "

"I suppose you get some storms here, being so close to the ocean."

"Yes, we do, but we're not right on the coast. Trevenston, though, gets some huge storms. Fielding House, being so far north gets snow. I worried about that when Alistair decided to have his wedding in December, but there was only a cold rain a day or two before." Standing up, I reached for my aunt's hand. "I thought we'd go into Hearthestone Vale after we leave here. We can shop and have lunch, and you can see the church in which I married, as did Alistair and Cecilia."

"And Prince Harry attended that one. I'd like that, since I wasn't invited," she uttered as we walked back through the graveyard to the golf cart.

***

"Disgraceful," my aunt huffed as we pulled out of the drive and passed several parked cars and one bus. Tours started at 10:00 a.m. and there was already a line of people queuing at the ticket booth.

In Hearthestone Vale, I showed her the church and then treated her to lunch at a pub. The *Thistle and Bell* was not a 'touristy' place, primarily because it was not easy to find. It was located below street level, so we took our time on the steep steps finally entering the low-beamed, white plaster and blackened-timber room that was partially filled with customers. No one even looked at us, which, to me, was quite all right. We took our seats at a battered table that had probably stood in the same place at least a century, but the pub was much older, dating back to the 1600s.

"Duchess, haven't seen you in here in a while," a man in his sixties wearing faded jeans and a heavy green work shirt said in greeting. "Is your American friend with you? He enjoys stopping in."

"I'm afraid not, Mr. Budball. He's in London working. I brought my aunt who is visiting from America to have lunch though. I told her on the way here that you serve the best fish and chips in town."

"That I do. One for each for you? Now, you know," he said directly to my aunt, "I don't serve them wrapped in newspaper."

"Newspaper? I should think not."

Mr. Budball and I laughed. I told him to bring us a plate each.

He stood there for a moment and then said, "Sometimes I see Lord Liam or Lady Aisling and her gentleman when they are at Fielding House. Always good to come say hello and have a pint, Lord Liam is. His Grace rarely stops by these days." He shook his head. "He's missed in the town. Her Grace, the young one, is too. Don't see her at all. Does her shopping in London and Paris, I hear."

Based on what I'd heard last night, this tidbit of information wasn't surprising. Will and I had always tried to do business in Hearthestone Vale, at least as much as we could.

"No mushy peas," I called out as he walked away.

"I remember." Being a local *and* a duchess meant I got the owner instead of one of his staff, not that they weren't nice, but Mr. Budball wasn't intimidated by titles and always enjoyed visiting, which I liked. I'd even created a character in *The Celestial Cat* series loosely based on him and a pub that was something like the *Thistle and Bell*.

"Mushy peas?" my aunt asked. "Should I call out no 'swedes?'

"Swedes aren't part of what we ordered, but mushy green peas often are. I have never been able to become accustomed to them."

"Well, you never really liked beans or peas when you were younger. Your mother said it was a texture issue."

"I still struggle with that," I admitted.

"I noticed in Cornwall that you picked the peas out of the vegetables that were served and pushed them aside. I'd like to buy some little gifts for a few friends. The items I got in Port Tristan had a sea theme, and the ones in Tintagel Village were Arthurian in nature. I certainly don't want people to know that you have coffee mugs for sale in Fielding House's gift shop. That's embarrassing, although I do want one of the prints of Fielding House and some notecards with the house on them for myself."

"I'll get them for you on the way back," I offered. My aunt was something else. It was all right for *her* to have a print and some notecards, but not for her friends in Hilly Dale. I felt sure she would pass them off as having been made specially for her. Thinking about that made me laugh out loud.

"What's so funny?" she demanded.

"Oh, nothing. I was thinking about mushy peas."

"Really, Jessica, you're not a child. Now, what do you recommend I purchase in Hearthestone Vale?"

"I'll tell you what I don't recommend, because that will be easier. No foods, no beverages, no toiletries, no candles, no seeds. Those things are quite popular here." I threw the last one in because some of the shops sold flower seeds and I did not want my aunt to have any problems with a customs official here or in America. I didn't think she would, but you never knew these days.

"So, that leaves me trinkets or cards again, and I'm not sure I want glass."

"I told you before that if you find something like that, we can have it shipped."

Won't that be expensive?"

"I'll take care of it. I owe you after how you defended me to Damaris."

"That *awful* woman, but I liked your mother-in-law. She has class and spunk, and she's sensible."

"She's mellowed over the years. She was a handful at first." I remembered how I once thought that she and Jane-Ann would be formidable opponents locked in a gilded cage fight, but instead, they'd become allies, with Josephine even suggesting that the next time my aunt came for a visit she should stay at Raven's Roost with her and let the young people bicker among themselves.

Mr. Budball brought our meals which my aunt declared tasty after taking a bite of her fish.

"What about some woolens? Mittens, scarves and such? There's a wonderful little shop not far from here. It's called *Wool Ye Fancy This?* and it has all manner of fine wool items."

"Speaking of 'fancy,' fancy finding you in here." We looked up from our meals to see Jackson hovering over us, grinning.

"I should have asked you to join us but wasn't sure where you were. We wanted to leave before the tourists arrived."

"I *was* in the library looking over some material when a tour guide burst into the room where she proceeded to berate me for 'tampering with private Fielding-Smythe property.' When I tried to explain I was a houseguest, she refused to listen and called the guard. I was escorted out in front of a gaggle of sightseers who took my picture and then taken to an office set up in a *shed* where I had to wait with a guard until my identity was confirmed by Mr. Bailing. He kindly took me back to the library where I returned the documents to their proper location."

"Oh, I'm so very sorry," I said.

He held up a hand. "While I was doing *that*, the tour guide returned with her group." Jackson pulled out an old wooden chair and sat down before continuing, "Mr. Bailing, who was with me for my own protection, informed her that I *was* The Duke of Hearthe's guest. Well, that just made all the tourists take *more* pictures, and the tour guide was afraid she would lose her job."

"She won't. She was *doing* her job. After the amorous couple, Alistair informed all the guides that if they discovered anyone not part of the family in a room they were to call the guard at once."

"I was terribly embarrassed, Jessica."

Mr. Budball walked over just as the phrase "at least you had your clothes on" escaped my aunt's lips.

"Appears I missed a good story," he chuckled. "Another guest of yours, Duchess?" He eyed Jackson for a moment. "I remember you from last time. You're the history professor. We had a talk about this pub. You were here with His Grace and Lord Liam one evening."

"You, sir, have an excellent memory. I'll have what they are having, and if you'd please bring me whatever lager you think I would like. I need it after the morning I've had."

"Right away, sir."

"A beer in the middle of the day, Jackson?" My aunt looked thunderstruck. "Well, I never!"

"Of course you never. That's because Hilly Dale is in a dry county, Jane-Ann, and only a couple of establishments have a license to serve. I'm in England, and I want a lager with my fish and chips."

My aunt looked like she'd sucked on something sour, so I said, "Just enjoy your meal and let Jackson enjoy his when it arrives. How are those mushy peas?"

"You're correct, they're disgusting and unnecessary."

"So, how was your morning? Seen any good seats, Jane-Ann?"

I tried not to laugh but failed miserably. Jackson couldn't help himself either.

"How could you know about that? It was just three hours ago."

"I'm sorry. It was too good to keep to myself. I texted him a photo of you taking a picture of where His Royal Highness sat."

"*Jessica*, how could you?"

***

That night, after Beck and I'd discussed the plans for his weekend visit to Fielding House, he asked how my aunt was enjoying Hearthestone Vale.

"She saw some of it, today. I took her to a pub."

"You took Miss Prim and Proper, the Hilly Dale Society Matron to an English pub? I wish I'd been there."

"She got her first taste of mushy peas at *Thistle and Bell*. What appalled her most was that Jackson had a lager with his meal. It was the middle of the day, you know."

"Jane-Ann isn't a stranger to alcohol. She ordered wine with her meal when she dined at my restaurant…only in the evening, of course, which is when we served it."

"She went to *dinner* there?" I never thought of my aunt going to Beck's restaurant at night. It had a more romantic feel to it in the evening and the dinner menu was expensive for Hilly Dale.

"Yeah, for a few months before I moved to New York, her book club would have an early dinner prior to their meeting. Margo Hunter got tiddly sometimes."

"Tiddly? Beck, are you picking up some of our expressions?"

"Well, in truth she got shit-faced once or twice, but I was trying to be discreet."

I laughed so hard that I was on the verge of crying. "Margo Hunter? Shit-faced drunk. She seems so stuffy."

"Believe me, she's not, and I'll say no more about it."

"Restauranteur/Customer Confidentiality?"

"Something like that. Seriously, she tried to pinch my butt once."

"Did she succeed?"

"No. I twisted and she got my hip. Fortunately, it was about 5:30 and they were the only customers. That book club meets early."

"I remember. 7:00 p.m."

"Looking forward to seeing you tomorrow. I'm taking off work early, so I should be there in time for dinner."

"Alistair got Liam a plane ticket home, and Aisling's taking the train, so she'll be here late, naturally. See you tomorrow."

Chapter Thirteen

Saturday morning, after breakfast, Alistair said, "Liam and I are treating Jackson and Beck to *Thistle and Bell* for lunch. Think you can handle Cecilia, Damaris, and Aunt Jane-Ann, Mum?"

"Check in with me later to see if we need medics," I teased, as the four of them were about to walk out to the Land Rover.

"I'm sorry. I know you didn't want to cancel Aunt Jane-Ann's party, but it might have been best had you done so," Alistair said.

"No, this is not her fault. This was planned some time ago. We have invited guests, some of whom arrived at Mayberry Hall last night."

"Shall we do the 'ignore, ignore, ignore?'" Liam suggested grinning "Or should we let everyone have a go?"

"This isn't a joke. Damaris was unkind to your aunt, and to me."

"I know. She's up herself. I'm just glad Alistair allowed me home for the party, and that Jordan will be here this afternoon." He punched his brother's arm like he did when they were children."

"Ouch!"

"She's glad you're going to be here," Beck said. "Let's go. Jackson and I are hungry after roaming around the estate this morning. Have a good lunch," he whispered as he passed me.

***

"Aisling, what are your plans this summer?" my aunt asked during our Saturday lunch of chilled salmon, salad and cold, roasted potatoes sprinkled with rosemary.

"I'm not certain. My friend Gemma's relatives have a house in Norway and some of us thought we might go there for a couple of weeks."

"Norway? You approve of this, Jes…Carola?"

"She's nearly twenty-two. I can hardly stop her from holidaying with friends, and Gemma is Elsie's daughter."

"But Norway when there are so many nice places to go in England, at least what I've seen of the country. Why there?"

At least it's not Mustique, I wanted to say.

"I've never been to Norway," Aisling replied, and tucked into her salad.

My aunt didn't pursue that and instead addressed me. "Something that's been troubling is that Beckham is here this weekend. If the two of you love each other so much, and he crossed the ocean for you and took up residence in a foreign country, why haven't the two of you married?"

Why she asked that question publicly, I have no idea. Before I could respond, Damaris said smartly, "She'd lose her title if she married him."

"Is this true? Would you lose your title?"

I glared at Damaris and then answered my aunt. "Yes, I would lose it, but that's NOT the reason, Aunt Jane-Ann. I'd rather not discuss my relationship with Beck, if you don't mind."

We ate in silence until Damaris asked, "What time must I be ready for tonight, Cecilia?"

"Oh, I think…ouch! Who kicked me?"

"I apologize, dear Cecilia, I mistook your foot for the napkin I dropped," Aisling replied in a sticky-sweet voice.

"It hurt!" She leaned down for a moment to massage her shin. "At least my evening dress will cover the bruise," she announced after she righted herself. "To answer your question, Mummy, everyone's going to be here at 7:00. You know it *has* to be an early party." Cecilia looked at my aunt. "Josephine will be here, too."

"What's that? A party?" Aunt Jane-Ann looked puzzled. "You didn't tell me there was going to be a party tonight, Jessica."

"Thank you, Damaris, for bringing it up just at this moment, and you, Cecilia, for announcing it." I turned to my aunt, "It appears I was remiss in not telling you about your *surprise* party."

Damaris, her dark eyes wide, cried in mock horror, "Oh, such a faux pas on my part, Mrs. Simmons. I do apologize. I forgot it was to be a surprise. Who *has* those parties these days anyway? Most I know wish to be prepared, so they will be dressed appropriately and not caught-out in some ragtag clothing." She glanced at my aunt, whose dark-green cardigan over a floral blouse was visible above the table.

"*We* were going to have a surprise party," Aisling snapped. "Until you brought it up."

"I did nothing of the sort. I merely asked what time a party was to be held."

"And Cecilia answered while looking at my aunt. What is *wrong* with the two of you?"

"Aisling, that's enough," I reprimanded.

"Mum, they're always spoiling things."

Once again, I had to say, "Not now," to one of my children. I leaned over and whispered "Manners."

"But they…"

"Not now."

"So you're throwing a party for me? I thought you had forgotten today was my birthday, but the trip was more than enough, and a such a surprise."

"No, I had not forgotten. The children and I planned a surprise party for you for tonight some time ago. We've invited friends to attend. Elsie and her husband will be here."

"And, of course, I've invited some of *our* friends," Cecilia added. "It should be quite the party, and all in *your* honor, Mrs. Simmons."

"Well, thank you. I *am* honored."

"As well you should be. A duchess is hosting it for you," Damaris replied, smiling at her daughter.

"Yes, *I* am," I stressed, forcing Damaris to direct her gaze to me.

"Of course, Carola, I meant you." Her lips tightened.

I gave her a dazzling smile. *Sure you did, you spiteful cow.* Like spending the night in an upstairs bedroom instead of The Duchess's Bedchamber, this was another instance of putting Damaris in her place. Just because her daughter was a duchess did not mean Cecilia was the only one present.

"Is the party grand?"

"It is only black-tie," Damaris put in, causing my aunt to flush in embarrassment. "Formal attire."

"I know what black-tie means. I didn't bring...I don't have..." she stammered. Cecilia gave her mother a side-eye, which I caught, and my daughter-in-law knew it.

"Don't worry about that, Aunt," I soothed, " I've got it under control."

"Aunt Jane-Ann, you will have such a good time preparing for this!" Aisling cried before taking a bite of one of Mrs. Sturge's homemade rolls. "Yummy, I've missed these rolls."

"Beck said Jordan was arriving later this afternoon," I said, buttering a piece of the bread.

"Yeah, she's coming in on the train. Liam is picking her up. They haven't seen each other in a few weeks, so they will want some time to..."

"Aisling," I warned, and then asked, "What time will James be here?"

"Oh, he's arriving with his father, and he's bringing his brother. I've asked some of my single friends to come. I hope that's all right."

"Aisling, you should have said something. Where are they going to stay?" Cecilia wanted to know. "The south wing where we sometimes house guests is now part of the tour, and it's not ready."

"I hadn't thought of that. Sorry," my daughter said and shrugged. "My friends won't care. It's just Gemma, Penelope, Amaranthia, Juliette and a couple of others. They are used to roughing it in old houses. Juliette and her brother even grew up in the family's rundown castle. You know the Pestleworth's, Mum. Lord Pestleworth's the..."

"I know of whom you speak. I know most of your friends, Aisling, but you really should have let Cecilia and Alistair know in advance," I chastised my daughter. "You're going to have to make reservations for your friends somewhere in Hearthestone Vale or cancel the plans."

"Me?"

"Yes, you didn't inform anyone, so you will need to take care of the matter. When you finish your lunch, unless you want to spend the afternoon helping some of the staff clean the rooms and change the linens in that side of the house, you had better start calling the B & Bs, but be prepared to check outside of town. Most of the guests we invited are staying at Mayberry Hall, so it will be booked. Also, remember it's Saturday and you know tourists visit this area on the weekends."

"I'll help the staff. I want my friends to stay here," she volunteered, which was more than my daughter-in-law would do.

"The staff has more to do than clean rooms for your friends," I pointed out. "Ring a few places nearby."

"But you said, unless I wanted to help the staff..."

"Yes, I did, but I wasn't serious. You can't really believe they would have time to do that work, today of all days."

"By the by, we closed Fielding House to tourists today," Cecilia announced. "I instructed a member of staff to put a sign just before the turn-off stating that the house is closed for a private party. So, you see, Carola, if you and your aunt *had* left the house for lunch, she would have seen the sign and inquired. Mummy and I didn't let the cat out of the bag after all." Cecilia gave a little smirk, daring me to say something further on the subject.

For Alistair's sake, I truly wanted to like Cecilia. I *had* liked her up until she married my son, or stepson as Damaris insisted. This change had to be due to her mother's interference. I just knew it.

***

While I was getting dressed for the party, there was a knock on my bedroom door. Opening it, I was delighted to find Beck standing there in black-tie, smiling at me. "May I come in?" he asked.

"Of course." Holding the door open, he stepped past me and into the room. "Don't you look handsome."

"Thanks." He took in my black bathrobe and slippers. "Is that what you're wearing?"

"I suppose I could make it work with a tiara. I know this is not really the norm for a birthday party, nor are tiaras the norm for black-tie events – white-tie, yes – but there are exceptions, even for royalty. The children and I decided we would do this for my aunt's birthday, and most attending love to dress for things like this and aren't bothered that it's not exactly 'proper wear.' The women enjoy..."

"Showing off their jewels?"

I laughed. "Perhaps. Aunt Jane-Ann told people in Hilly Dale that I walked around wearing gorgeous jewels. We wanted to make her fantasy of how the nobility live come to life."

"That's really nice, considering how she acted toward you in Arkansas, and from what you described, on this trip."

"I've come to learn more about my aunt on this holiday. Behind her traditional exterior and commanding personality is a woman who yearns for excitement. She had a difficult life with Ed, and I know she watched every penny. You should have seen her at the flower show, the church on this estate, and the church in Hearthestone Vale. She was ecstatic. Giddy even. So, I'm glad to make this holiday and her birthday special."

"And this is one of the many reasons I love you," Beck replied, planting a kiss on my forehead. "Oh, maybe I shouldn't have done that in here. This was your home with Will, and we kind of have this unsaid rule about PDA in places where your family..."

"It's all right. I learned quite a bit about myself while traveling with Jackson and Aunt Jane-Ann. I don't think Will or anyone – well, except maybe for my mother-in-law – would mind if we shared a kiss in front of them. Josephine *might* not because she's practical and lost her husband while she was near the age I was, and she's had some suitors since then, but out of respect for her, I'd prefer not to engage in any overt displays of affection."

"Agreed. How long ago were these *suitors*?" Beck asked, grinning.

"She's got one now, but he's only a baronet. Josephine descended from two great families - the Irish Butlers on her paternal side and the Howards on her English maternal one. It goes way back, of course, but she spent her part of her early life in Ireland. That's why she has a trace of an Irish accent. Their marriage would have been something of a scandal had her pedigree not been so established. Take note of Anne Boleyn's portrait in the Great Hall."

Beck gave me a blank look.

"Jackson can fill you in on the history of the families and such. Now, I've got to get dressed, so I can help Aunt Jane-Ann."

"Okay," he said, looking at clothes strewn across the sixteenth-century carved tester bed. "Come to think of it, I've never been in this room before. So, this is where all the duchesses slept at some point?" He eyed the messy bed again.

"I never did, until after Alistair married. He always insisted I stay in my old bedroom – The Duke's Bedchamber. Between you and me, I was happy when he decided to take it over. I'd really rather be in a guest room than in here."

"I'm pretty sure Damaris is seething that she's been relegated to the top floor with the likes of me, and now Jackson. He moved up there because Liam's here." Beck walked over and looked out the window. "You seem different. More...open, maybe."

I shrugged. "Perhaps."

"I'll let you get dressed, or I could help you..."

Laughing, I escorted him to the door. "Go on with you."

"Can't wait to see Jane-Ann's expression."

"It would have been better if Damaris and Cecilia hadn't spoiled the surprise. Damaris probably did it on purpose. She's a bitch."

"Jessica, your language," he imitated my aunt. "You usually just use 'cow' to describe Damaris."

"Get out and let me get dressed!" Laughing, I closed the door and locked it.

Chapter Fourteen

Jane-Ann Simmons, dressed in an A-line, ankle-length, gray, beaded-silk, Givenchy dress, and wearing the famed Fielding Larkspur tiara of diamonds and sapphires, entered the Great Hall on the arm of my tuxedo-clad son Alistair. Because my aunt had become such a fan of Masterpiece Theater and PBS television programs, I wanted to give her a *Downton Abbey*-style birthday party. Although the other women present were in full-length evening gowns. I'd chosen the ankle-length one for my aunt's safety. We could bend a 'rule' here and there. Couldn't have her tripping over a hem. Nevertheless, she looked elegant.

As they crossed the checkboard tile floor and approached the center of the room, the string quartet in the minstrels' gallery began the tune *Happy Birthday to You*, which was sung to her by a crowd of glamorously-attired men and women, most of whom she did not know. The crowd followed by singing a rousing round of *For She's A Jolly Good Fellow*. My aunt's face registered a mixture of fright and exaltation.

I stepped forward, mindful of my own plum-colored silk evening gown's hem and gave my aunt a kiss on the cheek. "Happy Birthday, Aunt Jane-Ann."

"Jessica, I mean Carola, what should I do?" she asked, grabbing my hand and letting go of Alistair's arm when Cecilia joined us. "Do I curtsy to everyone?"

"No. You curtsy to no one. Enjoy yourself. These people came to celebrate your birthday and to welcome you to England."

Cecilia, dressed in a pale-blue bespoke Dior evening gown, touched the all-diamond tiara she wore on her piled-up blonde hair. It might not have been the most beautiful tiara, but it *was* the most expensive one in the room. After taking Alistair's arm, she glanced at my aunt, gave a smile and turned to the guests. Before Alistair could open his mouth, Cecilia, with the air of a television presenter, announced, "Welcome everyone to Carola's aunt's eighty second birthday party."

To the friends and family gathered, Alistair appeared to be at ease, but I could tell by his slightly narrowed eyes and the tightening of his jaw that he was not happy with her. They obviously had not settled the issues that occurred the day we arrived. Now she was taking over. I heard him mutter, "She's my aunt, too, Ceci. Let me do the talking."

Cecilia gazed up at him, gave a smile, and then turned back to the guests, waving her arm in a 'go ahead' motion.

"Please welcome my aunt, Jane-Ann Simmons. She's visiting us for the first time from Hilly Dale, Arkansas, where my *mother*," he paused and looked at me, "grew up. I hope you will all ensure that my aunt has a wonderful time this evening and help her celebrate her birthday." This time he looked at Damaris. "I've opened the south wing for tonight's celebrations. A buffet has been laid in the formal dining room. Thank you for coming tonight and joining us for this special evening." He lifted the back of my aunt's hand to his lips and bestowed a kiss. "Happy Birthday, Aunt."

"Alistair, that was beautiful," she said softly, tears welling. "I never dreamed something like this was possible."

"We are certainly pleased you approve, Mrs. Simmons." Cecilia touched her tiara again, and in consternation looked at the one my aunt had borrowed. I'd gone straight to Alistair about selecting one for her, and he had wholeheartedly approved the one I had in mind. Cecilia apparently had not. I noticed her mother was not wearing one. She wasn't entitled to wear one of ours, but neither was my aunt. He could have been generous as he'd been with Aunt Jane-Ann but must have thought Damaris might abscond with it. At the least, she'd have been certain to be photographed in it and that picture along with a detailed description, including the value, would be mentioned in an article.

"Please call me Aunt Jane-Ann," I heard her say to Cecilia.

"If you wish." Once again, Cecilia did not suggest my aunt refer to her by her given name, but at least she hadn't yet told her to call her 'Duchess' or 'Your Grace.' That would not have worked in Cecilia's favor.

Josephine, looking regal in own family's tiara of clover-shaped emeralds surrounded by diamonds, and wearing an ankle-length dress made of pale-green silk damask joined us, sparing further awkwardness. To my surprise, Beck was escorting her.

"I met her when she was entering the front door," he told me when we stepped aside so that Josephine could speak with my aunt.

"What were you doing near the front door?" I inquired.

"Thinking of bolting," he answered. Seeing my surprise, he amended, "I wanted to step away from this for a moment. To you, it's nothing. To me...well, I feel like an outsider. It's my first formal party here. Oh, I've been to black-tie events in New York, but this is out-of-my-league. Dukes and Duchesses. Earls and Countesses. Lords and Ladies. Even Aisling and Liam have titles. God, even little William Charles is an earl! I'm just a guy from Hilly Dale."

"This is a small gathering of friends and family. You're definitely not an outsider, at least not to those who count."

"But there are some who think so, right?"

"There are at least a couple here who think I am, and I became a countess when I was nearly twenty-five and a duchess about four years later. No one expected *that* to happen, for several reasons."

"You fit in perfectly, and even Jackson moves with ease among these people."

"I'm used to it. Jackson fits in because he knows the history of some of the people's families that are present and converses about that, which both flatters and impresses them. Teaching has helped him overcome any insecurities he might have had. I'm surprised you feel this way. You've never had a confidence problem."

"I've never been among the type of people with whom you associate. It's intimidating," he confessed. "This just brings home to me how much you changed when you left Hilly Dale and how difficult it was when you returned there."

"If PDA wasn't frowned upon, I'd grab you and plant a big kiss on your lips right now." I gave him a kittenish look and bit my lower lip.

"See, there are all these rules I don't know," he mumbled, completely missing my flirtation.

"One rule is that I need to return to my aunt. You know Liam, Alistair, and Jackson. They will introduce you to some people. If you fancy meeting the younger set, there's always Aisling and Jordan.

They might let you hang around with them," I teased. "I have to play hostess."

"Very funny. It's weird seeing Jordan at something like this. I'd take a photo and send it to her mother, but I think I'd better not. She'd be pleased, but Bianca might just fly over here and butt in, and you've got enough of that with *her*." He nodded toward Damaris in a floor-length pale-yellow number who was flirting with the Earl of Cradleburn.

Poor man, his wife had died last year and Damaris was moving in on him. Maybe I'd tell my aunt that a *married* woman was after a man at the party, and maybe I'd tell her it was Damaris. I couldn't do that, but the thought cheered me.

"Earth to Jessica," Beck said snapping his fingers. "What are you thinking?"

"Something naughty."

"Sounds fun. Go hostess. I'll try not to embarrass you with my attempts at conversation with the elite."

"You would never do that. Josephine likes you or she wouldn't have allowed you to escort her into the party. She's a hard-sell. It took me *years* to establish a relationship with her."

"She complained that Alistair or Liam should have done the honors."

"Well, one of them should have, but Josephine didn't arrive on time, and Alistair was escorting my aunt. Liam was somewhere canoodling with Jordan."

"Don't say that! I like Liam, but 'canoodling' sounds like something your aunt would use to describe…well, I don't even want to think about *that*."

"She does use that word. Look, Jackson's stepped in to help Lord Cradleburn with Damaris. Maybe you could join them and send Damaris on to someone else."

"Mrs. Simmons, it is an honor to celebrate your eighty-second birthday here at Fielding House," Josephine was saying when I walked up, and it was just in the nick of time. I swear I thought my aunt was going to curtsy to my mother-in-law, but she remembered and graciously thanked her for attending.

"I wouldn't have missed it, Jane-Ann. I myself turned eighty-two a few years ago, and there's life still left in me." She leaned closer. "I'm still dating. He's just a baronet, but there are not too many choices at this age, but, he'll do."

My aunt's mouth opened and closed. I wasn't sure if it was in admiration or horror at Josephine's revelation.

"Oh Aunt Jane-Ann, you look beautiful," Aisling cried, interrupting her grandmother and giving her great-aunt a hug.

"Please be careful, Aisling. I don't want this tiara to fall off my head and break," my aunt replied. At that moment, she reminded me of her sister - my mother - standing in my room at Mayberry Hall while I was dressing for my wedding. She'd said almost the same thing to me.

"It won't," I promised, reaching up to check the sapphire and diamond tiara. The tiara was one of the oldest and most beautiful in the Fielding-Smythe collection. After I assured her it was secure, I made certain of my own. I was wearing my favorite aquamarine and diamond bandeau that I wore at my wedding and at Alistair and Cecilia's.

"And what about me?" Josephine asked, presenting her cheek for Aisling to kiss.

"Sorry, Nan. Delighted you could attend."

Jane-Ann and Josephine tried to engage my daughter in conversation, but Aisling was distracted by the sight of her boyfriend James Walkstone, Lord Cradleburn's youngest son, talking to an auburn-haired girl wearing a decidedly inappropriate gown. She was standing close to him, occasionally touching his arm.

"Go on with you, Aisling," Josephine said, giving her granddaughter a push. "Go to your young man. Don't let that strumpet get her hands on him."

"Strumpet!" Aunt Jane-Ann was on alert. "Strumpet!" My aunt was always on the lookout for improper, or in her viewpoint, immoral behavior, hence my thought about Damaris moving in on Lord Cradleburn.

"Yes, look at her spilling out of the neckline of that long, tight, black dress, and at a formal party in the residence of a duke. I know her aunt's little more than a gossip-monger. Friend of Damaris

Hempstead. Writes a column about what she thinks occurs in upper class lives. Allensworth is her name."

"I met her." Aunt Jane-Ann was in her element regaling Josephine of the encounter with Isabel Allensworth at The Chelsea Flower Show, which started Josephine on the subject of Cecilia not attending...again.

At just the right moment, Elsie joined us. When my mother-in-law and aunt paused in their conversation, I jumped in. "Lady Toddle, you know my mother-in-law, the duchess."

"Duchess, how nice to see you again."

"Lady Toddle," was her reply.

"And of course, you remember my aunt from the flower show."

"Please excuse me. I'd like to speak to Alistair about that young woman who was talking with Aisling's young man," Josephine said and walked as quickly as she could across the room.

"She seems so intent on getting information about a young woman with whom Liam was speaking a moment ago."

"I'm certain she's talking about Aubergine Olivier," Elsie said.

"WHO?" my aunt and I asked in unison.

"Aubergine Olivier. Yes, it's a worse name than 'Elsie.' I'd rather have been named for the family's first cow than an eggplant. And do you know her family claims to be related to the great Laurence?"

"Very distantly, I'd imagine." I was glad the young woman had moved on to someone else who seemed to be enjoying her attentions.

"Mrs. Simmons, how was your time in Cornwall? Did you enjoy The Eden Project?" Elsie asked.

"Oh, Lady Toddle, I'm so happy to see another familiar face here. The Eden Project was interesting. I much preferred The Chelsea Flower Show, though."

"I do, too," whispered my friend, "but don't tell anyone, and please remember I've asked you to call me Elsie."

With both women laughing and talking, I wandered over to Alistair, after seeing my mother-in-law was no longer with him. "Are things all right? I noticed you seemed a bit tense."

"Only you, Mum, would notice that," he replied. "Nan was going on about Aubergine and James. I didn't invite her. I can only assume

Cecilia did. She's one of *her* friends. James is too smart to lose Aisling for that old piece."

"Alistair! You shouldn't refer to Ms. Olivier that way."

"Sorry. She is one though. Not that I know first-hand, but she wants to marry a title and is willing to do anything to get one. She's older than she looks."

"Then she shouldn't have been chatting-up James. He may have a title, but he's the youngest son, so he's not going to be an earl."

"And I'm the highest rank here, and I'm...married," he said, looking around the room. "Have you seen Ceci?"

"Not for a while, but I wasn't looking. I see Damaris's husband isn't here though. What is happening there?"

"Everton seems to have had a pressing engagement in London and couldn't attend."

"Well, I'm surprised that he didn't want to attend, if only to see if he could lure some of our guests into putting money in his bank."

"I think it was more of an 'I don't want to be around Damaris at the mo' type of engagement."

"I've always thought Everton to be rather greedy and sneaky, Alistair. I know your father didn't wish to do business with him, and I never believed he was that against Damaris having a reality show."

"Ceci said he was extremely against it. Threatened divorce. Old Poleduck's not thrilled with him. I'll tell you that much. Cecilia wants me to put a little money in his bank so he can capitalize on my rank."

Horrified, I asked, "You're not going to do that, are you?"

"I couldn't if I wanted to. You know Poleduck, and besides, I agree with Father and you."

"More socializing for both of us. Do check on your aunt occasionally and make sure she's having a good time. I don't want her to think I'm hovering."

"This was a lovely gesture, Mum. I know you haven't seen eye-to-eye with Aunt Jane-Ann, and she made your life in Hilly Dale difficult."

"I realized that Aunt Jane-Ann just wanted to belong and had been hanging on my mother's coattails most of her life. I felt she deserved some happiness and ease in her later years, and now with the house and her holiday, she'll be Queen Bee of Hilly Dale when she returns. Thank you for allowing her to wear that tiara tonight. I know it's not traditional for someone like my aunt to wear one, especially the Fielding Larkspur."

"Like you, I wanted to make this evening special for her. Ceci gave me a time over it. Her own mother isn't able to borrow one. Of course, she felt her own mother took precedence to a relative of my stepmother's. I wish Father would have let you adopt me."

"He wanted to, but your mother, Andrea, wouldn't relinquish her rights."

"I can believe that. Onward we mingle. Thanks, Mum."

I took a glass of champagne from a passing server and wandered around the Great Hall, stopping to talk briefly or catching snippets of conversation as I passed by and occasionally making a comment. *Only a few minutes each is sufficient.* Josephine had trained me well.

"I'm telling you Lord Cradleburn, it's been such a delight visiting England and living like the English do," Jackson was saying as I joined them.

"Well, I wouldn't say it is exactly like most do here," the earl replied, laughing. "We may appear fortunate, but our country homes need repairs; our townhomes need repairs. Everything is extremely old. It's no wonder the children want more modern places. My youngest, James, doesn't want anything from the houses. Good thing, Jago is inheriting."

I waited for a pause and said, "I hope you are both enjoying the evening."

"Carola! Didn't see you standing there," Lord Cradleburn cried. "Wonderful party."

"You and Jackson must be having an interesting conversation."

"Yes, we are," Jackson cried. "We've discovered a love of history. We were just discussing how young people have no interest in it and want everything modern."

"I caught the end of that when I walked up."

"I'm delighted to see James has found a lovely girl in Aisling. She does you and William credit."

"Thank you," I said, taking in Aisling's simple, lavender, flowy ankle-length dress. Her shining blonde hair was held back from her face by two diamond barrettes and I'd gifted her the pair of amethyst and diamond earrings she was wearing. Will had given them to me on our fifth anniversary.

"I hope she and James can maintain a long-distance relationship now that he's finished at St. Andrews. He's going to be working for an investment company in London. What's the name of Mr. Hailey's firm?"

"Courtney Hazelforth."

"That's the one! Now, have you and Mr. Hailey set a date?"

"Oh, I think things are still new, and, of course Beckham hasn't been in England long," Jackson casually commented.

"I really must speak to other guests. Lovely to see you, Arthur," I answered, using the earl's given name.

Beck was standing with Jordan and Liam directly under the portraits of Elizabeth I, Henry VIII, and Anne Boleyn. I hadn't had a chance to speak with Jordan yet. She and my handsome son made a very attractive couple.

"Jordan! I am so glad you could be here." I took in her ruby-red, strapless dress that swept her ankles, her dark hair slicked back into a chic bun, and her simple gold butterfly necklace. "You look beautiful!"

"Doesn't she," Liam remarked.

Jordan's blue eyes sparkled as she looked up at him. "He's biased, and before you say a word, Dad, so are you."

"Guilty," Beck said. "Jessie…Carola, is Jane-Ann having fun?"

"I believe she is, but she hasn't said."

"She's having a marvelous time, Beckham," Jackson said walking up. "Here," he handed Beck a glass of champagne. "Looks like yours is empty." He took the empty one and gave it to a server passing by. "Jane-Ann told me she feels just like she's living in a different age, and believe me, this house has that effect on me too. I'm not fond of the Mozart the quartet is playing. It doesn't go with the house."

"I'd asked for Elizabethan or Tudor tunes just for you," I teased, "but this particular string quartet doesn't play those."

"So, I take it you're having a good time." Beck grinned. "You and that earl were having a long discussion.

"We were, and Liam, you would have particularly enjoyed it. Lots of gruesome tales of battles and revenge plots between some of the guests' ancestors."

"No *doubt*. James never wants to talk about things like that, but he's a decent sort and Aisling likes him. Look at them." Liam raised his hand, but I pushed it down. "I know, Mum, it's impolite to point, but they are over there and seem pretty cozy to me."

Aisling and James Walkstone stood with their heads close together. Jago, James' eldest brother and heir to the earldom, stood with them, but I noticed he was eyeing Jordan..

I didn't know Jago, but he reminded me of a character I'd written in my *Secrets of Snowdonia* series – the quintessential villain, devilishly-handsome who took what he wanted. In that case, it was a bejeweled, golden dagger from the fifteenth-century found stuck in the back of a librarian. My female protagonist had traveled back in time to learn the provenance and run into said villain back then too. In the present case, it appeared that Jago wanted Jordan. I wondered if Liam was aware...or Jordan. 'Shagger' Aisling had called him. I could see what she meant. No wonder she warned Alistair to get Liam home

"Oh yes, I've met some very interesting people, Beckham. Several of them are direct descendants of..." he paused for a moment. "Has the buffet started? There are less people in here."

"I imagine so. It's not a served meal," I replied. "If you are hungry, go ahead. I'll join you."

We had just taken a few steps when Mr. Bailing appeared and announced, "My Lords, Ladies, and Gentleman, Her Grace has asked that you join us in the south wing drawing room. If you will please follow me."

Several people in the room looked at me and then at Josephine who was still talking to my aunt. "To which 'Her Grace' is he referring?" Jackson asked.

"What on earth? Did you plan something, Mum?"

"No, perhaps Alistair and Cecilia planned something."

"Well, let's go see then." Beck took my arm and our group followed everyone else into the drawing room.

Chapter Fifteen

All the ropes protecting the sixteenth-century furnishings had been removed. The deep-red velvet drapes were closed, and the eighteenth-century chandeliers cast a soft glow over the guests. The portraits of long-dead Fielding-Smythes in various centuries' attire stared down at us as we entered and stood near the back of the room.

"Your Grace," Mr. Bailing addressed Alistair, "Everyone is present."

"Where are my mother, brother, and sister, Bailing? They should have seats." he demanded, looking around, finally seeing us standing at the back with Beck, Jackson, Jordan, and James Walkstone.

"It is all right, Mr. Bailing," I answered. "We are fine where we are. I trust this won't take long."

Cecilia stood in front of a large, white screen. I glanced at Alistair who stood next to a seated Aunt Jane-Ann and Josephine. He put his hands on both their shoulders and stared at his wife.

"Now that everyone's here, my mother has an announcement," Cecilia cried excitedly.

Damaris joined her. "I understand that this is a special celebration for Carola's aunt, but I have some wonderful news to share, and what better time than among friends and family.

Oh goodness. Cecilia's pregnant. What an inappropriate time to announce this, and before the immediate family even knows, I thought.

"Friends, my reality show has been accepted! *Wives and Girlfriends of the Nobility* has been accepted! I know you all are so happy for me, and for Cecilia. She is the star. Oh, we haven't got any other wives yet, but we do have some girlfriends. Aubergine, where are you? Please join me."

I was surprised Aubergine could walk in that fishtail dress of hers, and God forbid she bend over. Either her front would pop out or her backside would split the seams, but she made it and was beaming beside Damaris. Two other blondes – one in a white, fitted gown, and the other in a deep blue one -walked to the front, their behinds swaying.

"We have a teaser for the first episode to show you. It's hilarious. It's called *A Hillybilly in Hearthestone Vale*!"

"Beck, how could she? I thought this 'Duchess of Hillbilly Dale' business was over. What on earth is this? Another rehash to get back at me for something?"

"Let's wait and see what this is before you say or do anything."

And watch we did. There was the scene from just a couple of days ago in the family living room. Aunt Jane-Ann was calling the hogs and William Charles was shown trying to say 'sooie.' The voice-over explained that this was Carola, Duchess of Hearthe's aunt. There was a shot of Alistair, The Duke of Hearthe, wearing the hog hat.

Interspersed with this were clips of Cecilia talking to Aubergine and Damaris about me, my aunt, and my hometown, making comparisons to entertainment there and their own social lives in London. I recognized Isabel Allensworth as one of the 'girlfriends.' Due to her profession and propensity to spread and create gossip, I had no clue *who* in my set would even date her. The final scene was once again my aunt calling the hogs three times, and then a shot of the portrait of Elizabeth I and a few portraits of stern-looking men and women, with the voice-over saying "You can hear the hillbilly cry echoing in the halls of Fielding House. I wonder what *they* think?"

Except for the applause from the women standing near the screen, the room was silent.

"Isn't this darling!" Damaris cried. "William Charles is adorable."

Oh. My. God. I couldn't see my aunt's face, and I couldn't see Alistair's either, but I did see him reach over and put his arm around her as she bent her head.

"Well," I heard my mother-in-law say in a very sharp voice, "I don't know if it was entertaining, but it was certainly informative, Damaris. *I* learned quite a lot. We all have. Shall we all have a go at learning the cheer from our guest? I'll help her. I learned it the other day when this…video was apparently made. I believe I can lead it."

My mother-in-law in her tiara, diamonds, and silk stood up, marched to the front of the room, and cried "Pig Sooie" as loud as she could. Jackson led the applause and the room followed suit. By the fourth go-round, everyone had learned the cheer and appeared to be enjoying themselves. The Earl of Cradleburn was assisting an elegantly-attired female guest with the proper arm and finger movements.

"Thank you, Jane-Ann, for teaching us this amusing cheer. So much better than standing around talking and listening to a string quartet," Josephine declared. "Of course they are excellent at what they do, but they're not quite what I consider entertaining, but we all have different opinions on what we find *amusing*, don't we."

There was another round of applause from the assembled guests before Josephine looked directly at Damaris and said, "I notice you didn't join in, *Mrs.* Hempstead. Although, I believe this is an American hog call, I'd think 'sooie' would come *naturally* to you. Wasn't your great-grandfather a pig farmer?"

There was silence until Elsie's husband, Lord Alexander Toddle's voice rang out, "Damaris, did your great-grandfather call 'Pig hoo-o-o-o-ey' as the Wodehouse character tried to do when trying to get his sow who'd gone off her food to eat. What *was* that pig's name?"

"The Empress of Blandings," I helpfully blurted. I did have an English literature degree and a love of P.G. Wodehouse, as did my mother, so what better moment than to use my knowledge!

"Oh, thank you, Carola. That was also an American cry, wasn't it, so perhaps her great-grand had another type of call. Why don't you demonstrate it for us, Damaris? It would make a marvelous addition to your clip. Someone record this for her."

Elsie tried not to laugh out loud, but her head and shoulders were shaking so much her tiara was wobbling. Damaris stood front and center, trying very hard to retain her dignity and keep her mouth shut, which made me think this entire situation was being recorded for her tacky reality show, except the tables had turned, and not in her favor.

"I suppose she doesn't want to display further talents. It was only when your grandmother inherited that small farm -- oh, before you were born – and sold it that things changed for your family when she married someone with a good deal of money, I believe," Josephine enlightened us. "Am I correct. *Mrs.* Hempstead?"

126

"This is an outrage and invasion of my privacy," Damaris managed to sputter out. "My *daughter* is The Duchess of Hearthe, and I expect a modicum of respect. Cecilia, I don't know how you tolerate this family. No class at all."

"That's quite rich coming from you," Josephine said. "Jane-Ann, shall we take this party elsewhere?"

Alistair stood up and escorted my white-faced, slumping aunt to the back where I took her to the library. "Aunt Jane-Ann, I must apologize for the atrocious behavior of my mother-in-law."

Liam arrived with Josephine who came and sat beside my aunt.

"Will you ladies be all right? I need to speak to my wife," Alistair said coldly. "Liam, I'll need your help with the guests. See what we can salvage of this evening for them."

"Oh, I think they've been well entertained," Liam replied. "Damaris may not be particularly liked by most, but Cecilia...don't write her off yet. You don't know the whole story."

"I'm about to find out," my eldest son – yes, son – announced. "Come with me, Liam. I'll send Jackson and Beck to you, Mum, if you need them."

"I'm so embarrassed, Jessica. They were making fun of me," Aunt Jane-Ann said, struggling to remove her tiara. "This was all a joke. I'm a joke to them."

Removing her hands from the tiara, I said, "No, you are not. They were *supporting* you. Damaris is a bitch, and now everyone knows it."

"I concur," Josephine stated. "N.O.C.D."

"What's that?" asked my aunt.

"Not our class, dear," Josephine replied. "It's an old expression, but it certainly holds true for Damaris."

"It's a put-down, Aunt."

"N.O.C.D. I'll have to remember that, Jessica."

"Please don't use that," I begged. "It's not nice."

"No, it's not," Josephine said, "but I've kept quiet long enough. Alistair made a mistake. We all tried to discreetly warn him about Damaris and now that girl is nothing but a lazy, social-climbing strumpet. *I'm* the one who is embarrassed, Jane-Ann, by their behavior toward you, a guest, and toward Carola."

"You're very kind, Josephine, but I think I would like to go home. This isn't the place for me. It's my niece's home, but I don't belong here."

"We'll leave tomorrow for London and have a lovely time there," I said. "I am so sorry. This was supposed to be a wonderful evening for you."

"Jane-Ann, don't let this color your opinion of the family or the country. Don't think I didn't hear that Cecilia was behind those articles that came out about you while you were in the States, Carola."

"What?" I cried. "Wasn't it Damaris and Isabel Allensworth?"

"Interesting thing about being old, people forget you're there, or think you can't hear. I was present. Cecilia dragged the information out of Aisling and asked her to recite that poem at dinner. Aisling told her it was a secret and Cecilia agreed not to say anything, but as we were walking to the main hall, Cecilia, who was behind me called someone and shared the poem, I believe I heard her say 'Isabel.' It seems we've had a tabloid spy among us in the guise of Alistair's wife."

"I don't understand," I sat down...hard, and reached for my aunt's hand. "Cecilia? Surely you mean Damaris?"

"No, Carola, pay attention," she admonished me, sounding a lot like Aunt Jane-Ann. "But Damaris was certainly told."

And then it made sense. I remembered a phone call I'd had with Alistair when the news appeared online. I'd hated to ring him just a few days into his honeymoon, but I was concerned. He'd said Cecilia had been anxiously awaiting the write-up of their wedding and was devasted to discover that I, as Jessica Keasden, had been outed as Duchess of Hearthe and living in Hilly Dale, Arkansas. That was bad enough but the poem and other articles began appearing which ridiculed my new life in my home state.

Cecilia and her mother wanted to make me look a fool and push Cecilia into the limelight, but that hadn't garnered enough attention, and the bit about me being an author actually *helped* my career, and cast *me* into the spotlight, at least for a while. How that must have rankled, and it still must because I was getting invitations which Cecilia was not. However, she should have made more of an effort in her role as the Duchess of Hearthe.

I sounded like Aunt-Jane-Ann when I returned to Hilly Dale. She kept telling me I needed to try and fit in, but I rejected that. Somehow, though, I felt turning down a local garden club membership was nothing like refusing to attend things in Cecilia's husband's small *dukedom* and passing on things like The Chelsea Flower Show, and who knows what else.

Damaris, though, was behind the reality show. I was certain of that. She wanted to capitalize on the Fielding-Smythe ancestry and title no matter what. Beck was right about one thing. My daughter-in-law had indeed played a good game, and now there was little William Charles to tie her and her parents to the Fielding-Smythe family forever.

"I apologize, Carola for the shock," Josephine murmured, dragging me from further mulling my own theories, "but there's more. I believe that Damaris has been filming her little episodes for some time. Haven't you noticed that when you're here, she shows up and there's always some drama? When I'm here visiting alone, that woman *never* shows up."

Josephine might be right. I'd certainly seen it this visit. I couldn't imagine what was going through Alistair's mind at the moment. Anger over Damaris's behavior tonight, upset at Cecilia's potential complicity? Bewilderment? Hurt?

"Jessica," Beck said as he and Jackson entered the room. "Alistair needs you. We'll stay in here with Jane-Ann and Her Grace, if you like."

"Where is he?"

"You tell her what's going on, I'll stay with the duchess and Jane-Ann," Jackson volunteered.

Beck followed me into the hallway and closed the door. We walked a little farther west down the hall until we were in the old castle part with its stone floor and sconces that had candles burning in them tonight.

"What happened?" I asked, leaning against the cool stone wall.

The candlelight cast a shadow on Beck's face. "Alistair walked back in the room, took Cecilia's arm, and escorted her out so they could talk. They obviously didn't come back here."

"They probably went to the family wing or outside."

"After you left, Damaris kept trying to push her reality show on the guests, but other than the red-head, that Allensworth woman, and those other two women who acted like hangers-on, the rest went to the dining room and filled their plates. Is that normal?"

"For this set, yes. Ignore, ignore, ignore, but that doesn't mean they didn't care. They were embarrassed, and some disgusted by Damaris. Currently, the guests are letting us deal with our family matters privately, but most certainly supported my aunt, and helped turned the tables. You saw Lord Toddle's reaction. That helped immensely. What about Aisling and Jordan?"

"Liam and James took the girls outside. Aisling was crying."

I started walking back toward the main part of the wing. "Jessie," I heard Beck call, but I kept on until I reached the room where Aunt Jane-Ann was. I listened for a moment. Was that laughter? I tapped on the door and then entered. There was my aunt and my mother-in-law with tears running down their faces. Jackson had the oddest expression on his face.

"What's wrong?"

"Nothing's wrong, Carola," Josephine replied. "Everything is all right. While you were with Mr. Hailey, a number of the guests stopped by on the way to and from the dining room to say they thought Jane-Ann must be the most *excellent* aunt and so much fun. They said that other than the extremely common concept of a reality show featuring wives and girlfriends of the nobility *and* the equally common behavior of Damaris, that Jane-Ann teaching William Charles a cheer was adorable. His reaction was priceless."

"And then, and then..." my aunt tried to explain and burst into laughter, "and then when Elsie's husband and Josephine talked about pig farming and hog calls...oh my goodness gracious. At first, I was embarrassed, but then it suddenly seemed very funny. Josephine has said there is a television program called *The Blandings*. I must find the DVDs."

"Damaris came in to make some sort of dramatic apology to Jane-Ann claiming it was all in fun and she'd be a celebrity," Josephine said. "She also had a go at me for reminding everyone from whence she came."

"It was a mistake…" my aunt began.

"It was Damaris's mistake. There is nothing wrong with being descended from pig farmers, Carola, I may have come from a long line of Irish nobles and a few English ones, but that does *not* mean that *all* of them were great or noble. Why my great-great-great-great grandmother was a servant and her parents were what you might refer to as 'dirt famers.' She went into service at the age of eight. It is nothing to be ashamed of. It is simply that the pretentious Damaris has forgotten her family's origins and needed to be reminded and put in her place. I can assure you that Allensworth woman was taking notes. Oh, speak of the devil…"

In walked Isabel Allensworth. "I wanted to express my shock at Damaris's version of entertainment."

"Really? *You*? We were thinking you were taking notes," I snapped. "You're her friend."

"That's true, but I am first and foremost a journalist."

That was debatable.

My aunt sat up straight, looked the woman in the eye, and fully-composed, said, "Oh, I thought you wrote gossip and made up stories. *I'm* here on special assignment for my local *newspaper* to write about my trip and what it is like living among the nobility. I've certainly gotten an eyeful. Perhaps we should compare notes."

"I write a gossip column for tabloids, true, but at heart, I'm a journalist. I do research and I do have sources."

"Yes, your friends," I couldn't help saying. "Your spies."

"Now, that's quite unfair. I trusted Damaris. I've known her since our school days, but I will concede that she went too far this evening, and I'm happy to clear up a few matters."

And then Ms. Isabel Allensworth began to reveal what Cecilia and Damaris had been up to.

Aghast did not begin to cover my emotions after I'd heard the first one. "Excuse me for a moment, please."

Jackson walked out with me. Beck was waiting outside the door for me. "Jessica?" he queried, but the look on my face stopped him from saying anything else. I was going to put a stop to this right now.

"Jackson will explain everything!"

Storming down the hallway past the guests who were chatting and eating, I crossed in front of the large staircase behind the Great Hall and entered the family wing. Hearing voices from behind the door to the family living room, I threw it open. Cecilia, Damaris, and Alistair sat there. Cecilia was pleading with Alistair to forgive her, but by the look on his face, he was not ready to do that.

"Damaris, I'd like to have a quiet word with you...alone," I said in a flat voice.

"You can say anything in front of..."

"Very well. Alistair, I apologize in advance for what I'm about to say." Turning to look at my self-centered daughter-in-law and her spiteful mother, I lowered my voice and in a low tone said, "How *dare* you attempt to insult and embarrass my aunt – a woman in her eighties! Shame on you."

"It was meant to be amusing. You saw how the crowd reacted. They loved it and had a delightful time learning that ridiculous cheer."

"Damaris, is that how you see our friends and family, as a crowd to be entertained? Were we your test viewers? If so, you made a big mistake. They were appalled. They have class and were being polite and supportive after your stunt aimed at embarrassing an eighty-two-year-old woman, and most likely me as well. It didn't work, you know. You disgraced yourself."

"Mummy, I told you it wasn't nice. I apologize, Carola."

"I'm not the one to whom you need to apologize, Cecilia. My aunt would be the one, but I imagine she would laugh in your face, and if you're smart you will confess and apologize to Alistair and the rest of this family for the stunts you've pulled."

"Stunts? I don't know what you mean, Carola."

"If you won't share them with him, I will. I am certain you recall incident with the tour and young couple in the bed, Alistair."

"Yes," he replied.

"Carola, I'd be very careful what you say," Damaris warned.

"Why? Are you recording and taping this? Isn't that what you've been doing? That incident in the bedchamber was staged...staged by Cecilia for her mother's potential reality program, Alistair. *That* was the clip Damaris submitted. In fact, Isabel Allensworth is in with your grandmother and aunt at the moment filling them in on all the staging that's been done for Damaris's self-serving program, done at our family's expense and with Cecilia's help."

"That bedroom incident cost this family plenty, Cecilia, and for what? To help your mother with a distasteful, ludicrous program that tries to make families like mine look ridiculous." Alistair looked at his wife in disgust. "God! What else has been staged? Mum, please excuse me. I'm going to see Aunt Jane-Ann." He started for the door and turned to Damaris and Cecilia. "My aunt and my mother. You've insulted and attempted to humiliate both of them, and you recorded this family. I want you gone tonight. I'll have Mr. Bailing find a couple of rooms for you at one of the available places in the area. Don't expect Mayberry Hall. It's booked with family friends."

"Alistair, please...I'm sorry," Cecilia cried. "We need to talk. I promise this was not my idea."

Looked like Cecilia was going to throw her mother under the bus, but I knew my son was smart enough not to fall for that. This reality crap was something that took more than one to accomplish. We just needed to find out who else was involved at the house. My guess was the new staff that had been hired. Were they actors?

"Alistair, I'm William Charles's mother! I am The Duchess. I have a right to stay in this house," Cecilia screamed.

Alistair and I walked out and closed the door.

"Go upstairs, Mum, and tell Miss Hawkins that Cecilia is not to disturb William Charles tonight on my orders. I'm afraid she'll try to take him when they leave."

***

Early the next morning, I kissed Alistair and a sleepy William Charles goodbye. Aunt Jane-Ann fussed over the little boy who uttered a little 'sooie' thrilling her.

"Before you leave, I must apologize again for my wife and her mother, Aunt," he said. "Your birthday party was supposed to be special. I wanted you to enjoy it."

"It's all right, Alistair." Aunt Jane-Ann hugged him. "*You'll* be all right. I had a wonderful time despite their attempts to spoil it. Josephine and I are going to be *email* buddies. Imagine me being a pen-pal with a duchess! Just take care of the child. He's most important."

"Oh, don't worry about him. He will be fine. I'll make sure of that. I suspected Damaris was involved in trying to get you out of the way Mum," he said, his voice wavering slightly, "but I never thought Cecilia was and that she... she may have used me. I don't know what to say. I'm heartbroken. Mr. Bailing put them up at a hotel in Keswick last night."

"That far that late at night?"

"He drove them there himself. I've asked her to go home with Damaris for a while. She wants to take W.C., but I've refused to let her do that, and she doesn't dare cross me. I'm not even sure she really wanted a child."

My heart broke for him. "Alistair, do we need to talk privately? We can stay an extra day. I can even take William Charles to Lilac House if need be."

"I'll get the train back," Beck offered "and if Jackson and Jane-Ann want, they can go back with me, or I can drive them by car to London and you can return by train, if you feel you need to stay, Jessie."

"I know my way around London and can take Jane-Ann around," Jackson volunteered, "but I have a better idea. Beck we will drive you to the station in Hearthestone Vale, and then Jane-Ann and I will continue our holiday, with a little side-trip."

Alistair lifted his eyes and faced us. "Thank you all, but we'll talk later, Mum, when my head is clear. It's going to be all right. Aunt Jane-Ann is right. William Charles is the most important thing in the world to me. I'll see to things after meeting with Mr. Poleduck on Wednesday. I rang him this morning on his private number."

"Ring me any time." I gave him a kiss and placed another one on the top of William Charles's head. "Do what's best for you and for him."

"Thank you. Please don't mention any of the sordid details to Aisling and Liam. I know they witnessed a lot, but I don't want them to know about Cecilia's alleged deceit, just yet. I'll tell them when it's been decided what to do. It will come out. I don't trust Isabel Allensworth to keep this to herself. It's too…juicy, as Aisling would say."

I hugged and kissed him again, whispering "I love you" before I got in the car.

"Do you think they'll divorce?" Aunt Jane-Ann asked, as the four of us pulled away, this time with Beck driving my car to Hearthestone Vale.

"I don't know. Cecilia on her own wouldn't be an issue; they could work something out. With Damaris butting in and calling the shots for her daughter, and her banker father who has probably been chortling and rubbing his hands together ever since Alistair and Cecilia married, I wouldn't be surprised if they didn't try to get their hands on Fielding-Smythe money and gain full custody of William Charles."

"Could they?" my aunt screeched.

"The Fielding-Smythes have excellent attorneys and accountants who have the family interests in mind."

"I hope they do. That girl's mother is trash. I don't care who she is or how much money she has. Imagine treating *our* family as she did, and her own family was in *pigs*."

"There's money to be made in livestock. Alistair just purchased Highland cattle. Will judged shows, although I don't think he judged pigs."

"I should hope *not*."

We dropped Beck off at the train station and I took over the driving.

"Let's have a nice drive and enjoy the scenery." Jackson exclaimed. "I'm checking for hotels and B & Bs in the area of Highclere Castle right now. Be prepared for a visit to *Downton Abbey* and a stay in lovely country house hotel for the next couple of nights. My treat."

"Jackson?" I queried, after I pulled over at nearby motorway service station.

"Tomorrow we shall visit Highclere. It has a most fascinating Egyptian collection. You see, the fifth Earl of Caernarvon was an amateur Egyptologist who…" he paused. "Oh, it's not open yet."

"Let me make a quick phone call," I said. "I believe I can get us a private tour, Aunt Jane-Ann."

Chapter Sixteen

"So how do you think it went overall?" Beck asked as we drove to Lilac House Friday evening, two days after my aunt and Jackson left for America. I'd stayed in London after we returned from Hampshire because Alistair had come to town with William Charles for a few days while Cecilia and her mother were in Paris. He was still at the townhouse, but I wanted to go home, and Beck was agreeable, even if we did have to leave after he got off work. It was going to be late when we arrived in Broadway, but we hadn't spent much time together lately.

"The best I can offer is bittersweet. Jackson had a blast; my aunt had the trip of a lifetime, seeing things ordinary tourists wouldn't and getting caught up in a family drama, but the situation with Alistair and Cecilia is worrisome."

"Do you think they will divorce?"

"It's early days, but, yes, I think they will. I truly believe Alistair and William Charles will be much better off without Cecilia and her fame-hungry mother."

"A divorce will keep Damaris and Cecilia in the limelight, and maybe they *will* do a reality show, but I highly doubt anyone in Alistair's or your set would be a part of it. I guess all the Hempsteads are looking for a big pay-out if there's a divorce."

"I'm sure any financial windfall would be welcome, but I doubt it will be much, given the length of the marriage, and that Alistair would end up with full custody. She'll have the title, but as soon as she marries again, and she inevitably will because she's quite young, she'll lose that."

"You really think she set Alistair up?" Beck took a roundabout. "I still don't like these, especially at night. I've missed my turn on a few of the double ones."

"I know. It takes time. You must watch which lane you're in. I've ended up going to the wrong town because I went off the roundabout in the wrong direction."

"I do know which lane I'm supposed to be in," he replied, crankily. I knew he was tired. I was exhausted – physically and emotionally.

"All right then," I said, not wishing to upset him further. "As far as setting up Alistair, it's possible, since we know Damaris involved herself and was pushing her daughter to marry up. I imagine Cecilia upped her game after Will died."

"I'm sure she did! She and Damaris played their hand too soon, but he knew before they married that Damaris had tried to develop a reality show once before. This one, though…"

"I can't imagine many titled families would be interested in a reality show like that, or that their spouses' families would approve. Maybe girlfriends looking for notoriety or something would."

"Exactly, like Aubergine Olivier. She was an ex-girlfriend of Lord someone or other. I didn't know him. I have a feeling Cecilia would have been the only wife, and as a duchess *would* have been the 'Queen Bee' of the group, Damaris would have been right by her side giving advice to everyone and stirring up drama. Cecilia and that bedroom matter was disgraceful. I think that is what's pushing Alistair toward divorce. How could you trust someone who was setting up scenes for a television series without your knowledge. Who knows what was recorded or filmed for that matter. He hired a security company to check the house and property for hidden cameras."

"That would be illegal and Cecilia would be in some serious trouble."

"Alistair wouldn't press charges, but it would be something he could hold over her head in case the custody battle turns ugly. After the baby came, he indulged her, but he recently put a stop to things, or else Mr. Poleduck and Mr. Hartfield brought matters to his attention and explained that she was going through money right and left with her expenses for clothes, hotels, travel, and socializing. There's been trouble for some time, but I never talked about it. I think the push for a Mustique holiday was a mistake, and then the way she treated my aunt was the deal breaker.

"I was impressed by Jane-Ann's reaction to it all, and by the guests' behavior, and your mother-in-law and your aunt are acting like best friends."

"I'm glad about that. I was a little worried. Both are formidable women. Alistair told Aisling and Liam about everything this morning. I learned from them that neither was comfortable at Fielding House since Damaris was there so often. Aisling said she treated them with contempt. Although they are Will's children, they weren't the heirs and she commented often on how everything would be William Charles's one day. Don't tell Jordan, but Liam confessed he begged to be sent to Scotland and was taking his time. I know he planned for Jordan to join him during the summer though."

Beck yawned audibly.

"What makes me angriest is that Cecilia *used* all three of my children. Not only did she play Alistair, but she used Liam and Aisling, encouraging them to talk about my life in Hilly Dale. I suppose they didn't realize that the fall-out would create real problems there like what happened with Heather James. It was just meant to embarrass me."

"Uh huh," Beck mumbled and yawned again.

"I've about decided to forego the 'ignore, 'ignore, ignore' family policy and personally write a rebuttal to all of this and publish it."

"Jessie, STOP! No, you're not. Don't stoop to their level. Listen, you have talked about this most all the way from London, and now we've driven down your private lane and are parked in front of Lilac House and you haven't even noticed."

I looked up and there was my two-story, slate-roofed, honey-colored limestone house right in front of me. The light next to the front door was on and so were several inside. "Who is here? Aisling? I thought she and Gemma were planning a holiday after school term. It's not quite over. And Liam and Jordan left for Scotland."

"I asked your cleaner to stop by, tidy up, and bring Violet home."

"You did?"

"Yes. Now, do you want to keep worrying about these grown-ass adults who act like children, and your thirty-something-year-old stepson – son- who is capable of defending himself and hiring a team to help settle matters, or do you want to go inside, hug your cat, and spend some time with me?"

"You have to ask." I got out of the car and waited while Beck dragged the luggage from the car boot. "I'm sorry, Beck, for all this mess. I learned something from it, though. I learned that Will hid his title and wealth from me for a reason. He had to be sure I loved him for him."

"I'm sure that's true. Someone in his position has to be careful, and now Alistair's learned that lesson the hard way.

We walked up the front path. Taking out the key, I opened the door and stepped inside the flagstone entrance hall. There on the worn stairs sat my beautiful black Persian cat. Violet blinked her sea-green eyes at me three times in greeting before narrowing them and turning around and trotting upstairs with her tail sticking straight up. Then Beck pulled me to him and kissed me, and I forgot about everything but him and home, until we broke apart and he said, "So, your 50th is coming up in a few months. Where do you want to go?"

"Thanks for *reminding* me. Back to Cornwall."

"You're kidding me."

"No, I'm not, but I don't want to go to Trevenston. Let's go to the southern part. I've come up with the plot for the next *Harriet Donovan* and it's set in Cornwall."

"And?"

"Harriet's cranky aunt is visiting from Scotland and they've been invited to a wedding in Cornwall, and are staying at the bride's family's creaky, old manor that may or may not have a history of thievery in the past, and the daughter-in-law did it. The murder Harriet solves, I mean."

"Wonder where you got that idea."

"You know, I learned a lot on this holiday."

"Sounds like it."

I really had. Mark Twain was right when he wrote in *Tom Sawyer Abroad*, that you learned whether you loved or hated someone when you traveled with them. I had discovered I loved mine... both of them.

Epilogue

Jane-Ann Simmons, dressed in an azure Catherine Walker dress her niece had purchased for her in London held court in the living room of her large, white Victorian house in Hilly Dale, Arkansas.

"Ladies and gentlemen, I thank you for the applause. I so enjoyed presenting my program on The Chelsea Flower Show, and I'm delighted that Gatsby Gregson, Peter Franklin, and Amber Greene from *The Hilly Dale Gazette* could join us today. Unless there are any questions, tea will be served in the dining room."

There were questions galore as Jane-Ann knew there would be, but they weren't about her program. She'd been sure to give a brief account of her trip to England to visit her niece, to whet their appetites for more than that, and she'd sold her stories to the *Hilly Dale Gazette*, but she could still dish a little more without affecting that.

"So, you were at *The* Chelsea Flower Show with the queen, is that correct?" Gatsby confirmed.

"Oh, yes, Gatsby, and she was so charming. There we were just a few yards away from her, like I told you in our meeting the other day. Everyone, you'll just have to read the articles if you want to find out more about Cornwall, and Fielding House, and my personal, private tour of Highclere Castle my niece arranged. I tell you, it was an *experience*, but, of course, Hilly Dale does have its quaint charms."

"And you met other members of the nobility?" her friend Margaret Bosworth asked.

"Oh yes, quite a few. As you all know my niece Carola is a duchess."

"Carola? Peter Franklin looked puzzled for a moment until his wife Betsy Potter Franklin, nudged him.

"You know that's Jessica's middle name. She doesn't use it in England, unless it's for her novels."

"Oh, that's right. Please go on Jane-Ann."

"I met a couple of other duchesses at a party that was held in my honor, and I'm pen-pals with one." Her audience was enthralled. No need to tell them they were her niece's mother-in-law and ex-daughter-in-law. "Lady Toddle, a viscountess – she's my niece's best friend – was there with her husband. Oh, and I met a few earls." Why say one of them was her great-great nephew. "One was the Earl of Cradleburn. Pleasant fellow whose son is dating my great-niece, Lady Aisling. There were others there, too, *naturally*, and I met countesses as well."

"How exciting!" Catherine Coolcrane, a long-time member of the garden club cried. "To think, you were there wearing a gorgeous gown and you had on the most glorious tiara in the newspaper picture. Did you get to keep it?"

"Certainly not. That tiara was the Fielding Larkspur and made of diamonds and sapphires. It has been in the Fielding-Smythe family for a couple of centuries." *So, it wasn't quite that old*, she thought, *but near enough*.

"And did you really travel on a private jet?"

"Oh yes, but we had to return on commercial – first class, however," she said looking around to make sure everyone was listening and suitably impressed.

"Is your niece going to marry that handsome Beckham Hailey?" Margo Hunter asked.

"I'm ashamed to say that the answer is they are not."

"Are they still together?" Margo prodded.

"Yes, and while I don't approve. They have their reasons, which I understand. Beckham is applying to remain over there indefinitely."

"Doesn't his daughter go to school there?"

"Yes, and there may be a development there, but I'm not at liberty to speak of it right now, but when I know for sure, I shall certainly tell my closest friends. Before we have tea, I have one last thing to show you. Gatsby, will you please help me by getting something from behind the sofa?"

Jane-Ann stood up and waited while Gatsby withdrew a large, beautifully-framed color photograph of what looked to be small section of a church pew.

"This is a photo I took of where the Prince of Wales sat during my niece's husband's funeral." As expected, there were oohs and aahs. Jane-Ann beamed. "Yes, he sat right there, and the day I took this, *I* sat in the same spot!" She pulled out a smaller framed photo. "There I am in the exact seat."

"You sat where the future King of England sat?" Margaret confirmed.

"Yes. This was in an old church on my niece's family's estate. Lovely place. "Now, shall we have tea? I simply must tell you all the proper way to eat the scones. You know Cornwall and Devon have different ways of doing that, and speaking of Cornwall, and this is something you'll want for the paper, Peter and Gatsby, I went to Port Isaac. As most of you know, that's where *Doc Martin* is filmed and…"

The End

Author's Note

Thank you for reading *Aunt Jane-Ann Takes A Holiday*, the novella sequel to *The Duchess of Hillbilly Dale.* I hope you enjoyed it as much as I loved writing it.

Other books written by Jennifer Cadgwith

The Face Age

The Duchess of Hillbilly Dale

Made in the
USA
Monee, IL